REDEEMER
The Cross
Chronicles

Balogun Ojetade

DEDICATION

I dedicate this to My mother, Almeater Swan, who sparked my love for Science Fiction and Fantasy and to my sisters, Alesia and Phyllis, who taught me to read by giving me comic books, which made the love for Speculative Fiction that much deeper.

ACKNOWLEDGMENTS

I would like to thank my wife, Iyalogun Ojetade, for her support and my children – Osunyoyin, Koseefowokan, Bamitale, Okesina, Yetunde, Abiola, Oluade and Oriyemi – for being my muses.

I would also like to thank Milton Davis, a creative partner, jegna ("mentor") and friend for teaching me much and for producing Blacktastic work and sharing it with the world.

Finally, I'd like to thank my readers. Yeah...you...and you, too. This will *not* be yet another novel in which the author has thanked someone else and not you.
Uh-uh.
This thank you is, emphatically, for *you*!
Yes, *you*.
"Thank you! Thank you! Thank *you*!"
Now, read this book and then thank *me* for writing another masterpiece (smile).

CHAPTER ONE

Ezekiel Cross sipped cool, sweet water from a fresh, young coconut as he casually perused the glossy pages of 'American Music'. President Sim-Ming Bo smiled up at him from the magazine. The former U.S. Olympic Silver Medal gymnast, turned pop star and actress in Asia was now President of the United States. Ezekiel read the caption that ran across President Bo's small, round breasts – "President Sim-Ming Bo is all smiles as she begins her campaign for a second term in the White

House."

Ezekiel touched his index and middle fingers to his full lips. He kissed the tips of his fingers and then placed them on President Bo's smiling mouth. "You got my vote, Madam President."

He closed the magazine and tossed it into the cooler, which sat next to him in the white sand. He reached into the cooler and withdrew a small monocular.

Ezekiel looked through the monocular down the beach. A man and a woman were playfully splashing ocean water on each other's olive-toned bodies.

Ezekiel made mental checks as he studied the man – wavy, auburn hair, average height and build, deep suntan, a four-inch scar on his right calf, acquired during an exceptionally rigorous game of soccer.

The mark was confirmed. Ezekiel returned the monocular to

its place in the cooler and stood up, grabbing his white, linen shirt as he rose. He slipped the shirt on, but did not button it, leaving his lean, sinewy torso exposed. Against his mahogany skin, the shirt seemed even whiter.

Ezekiel studied his surroundings. A young woman and her son were nearby, tossing a Frisbee to their dog. The golden retriever would catch the floating disc in its mouth and return it to its masters, gleefully wagging its tail the whole while. They paid Ezekiel no mind.

He quickly reached into the cooler and pulled out a blue-steel .357 Sig Sauer pistol. Ezekiel thrust the gun into the waistband of his trousers. The steel cooled his back, comforting him. He took a deep breath and then walked along the shoreline, toward his mark, enjoying the tickle of the gentle waves as they washed over his sandaled toes.

The couple was now wrestling in the sand. Ezekiel smiled. They reminded him so much of himself and his wife, Mali, when they were the couple's age.

Mali loved to come to Myrtle Beach. She enjoyed the smell of the ocean, the sound of the crashing waves, the raucous conversation of the gulls. Ezekiel would describe the reflection of the drowning sun upon the water; how it gave the ocean a reddish-silver hue. Mali would smile, reaching out to feel Father Sun's warmth and Sister Wind's coolness, simultaneously, upon her palms.

They would have to take a vacation soon. It had been quite a while since they had escaped from the bustle of the big city. Ezekiel no longer loved Atlanta. It had now surpassed Chicago in population and New York in meanness. He only remained because of his loyalty to The Family.

The couple noticed Ezekiel's approach and ceased their playful grappling. They stood up. The woman grabbed the man's hand and held it tightly, rubbing his knuckles gently with her thumb.

Ezekiel smiled warmly. "Hello, there!"

The woman rewarded Ezekiel's smile with one of her own. "Hi!"

"Can we help you, sir?" the man asked.

Ezekiel sensed a hint of caution in his voice. He extended his right hand toward the man, who slowly grabbed it. Ezekiel shook the man's hand briskly. "I'm Ezekiel Cross. And you are?"

"I'm Sam," the man replied. "And this is my wife Regina."

Ezekiel shook the woman's hand. It was soft and delicate.

"I was wondering if you saw a woman walk by here," Ezekiel said, looking around and craning his neck as if searching for someone. "Gorgeous…tall…looks like she's in her mid-twenties, but she's really in her early forties."

Ezekiel laughed. The couple smiled and relaxed a bit.

"My wife would *kill* me if she knew I said that!" Ezekiel chuckled.

"I'll be sure to tell her when I see her," the woman replied, giggling.

"No! Don't do that!"

Ezekiel laughed with the couple.

"The only gorgeous woman I've seen on this beach today is my wife," the man said, kissing his wife's hand.

"*Gotta* be newlyweds," Ezekiel replied.

"How can you tell?" the man inquired.

"By how close you're standing

next to each other," Ezekiel began. "The way you kissed her hand just now…and the fact that every time she looks at you she smiles."

"Oh, your wife must smile for you," the woman said. "You're a charmer."

"From time to time," Ezekiel replied. "We've been together since high school."

"Well, we've been married for five days," the man said.

"How have you and your wife managed to stay together as long as you have?" the woman asked.

"By being honest with each other at all times and having open channels of communication," Ezekiel lied. Actually, his relationship with his wife had lasted so long because Mali had put up with his secrets. She never questioned why he would be gone for days at a time; why he owned two cell-phones – one whose

number she did not know – and why
he owned an arsenal of firearms
and explosives. He was good to
Mali, to his mother and to her
parents. For her, that was enough.

"We should last forever,
then," the man said. "We tell
each other everything."

"Everything?" Ezekiel asked,
feigning shock.

"Everything!" the man said
assuredly.

"Then, when are you gonna
tell her your name is really
Griffin McMahon?" Ezekiel asked,
smiling.

Griffin's proud expression
faded. The woman grabbed his hand
again and squeezed tightly.

"What's wrong, Diana?"
Ezekiel inquired. "You look like
you've seen a ghost."

"Please, don't hurt us,"
Diana pleaded.

"I…I have money," Griffin stuttered. "I'll pay you *double* what they paid you to do this."

"Look, Griffin," Ezekiel began. "I like you. I really do. I have been studying you for weeks now. You seem to be a good guy who just ended up crossing the wrong folks."

Griffin snatched his hand away from his wife. Tears streamed down his cheeks and fell from his chin, making tiny dots in the sand. "Go, baby! He doesn't want you. Go!"

"No," Diana shouted. "I will not leave you here!"

"They wanted me to sell little girls into prostitution and slavery, did you know that?" Griffin asked Ezekiel. The tears increased, leaving puddles at his feet. from a drizzle to a torrential rain.

"I can't hear this," Ezekiel said. "Not my concern."

"The girls were no older than twelve," Griffin continued.

Ezekiel shook his head. "Not my concern."

"They take those little girls and they…"

The calm, cool air exploded.

Griffin crumpled to the ground.

The white sand reddened as blood poured from the chasm in the back of Griffin's skull.

Diana screamed a scream so full of despair and anguish that it gave Ezekiel chills. The assassin took a deep breath and fired again. The screams stopped.

Ezekiel looked down at the couple who – moments before – was so full of life, so full of laughter and hope, and reminded him of himself and his beloved Mali.

"That's it," he whispered.

"I'm out."

The Family – and Atlanta – would just have to do without him.

CHAPTER TWO

Cascade Road was quiet. It was Sunday evening, so most of the shops, spas, and coffeehouses were closed.

Ezekiel turned onto Wilson Drive and then into his driveway. With the flip of a switch on the dashboard of his Range Rover, the garage door came to life and the door slowly ascended. He pulled the SUV inside the garage and walked into the house.

A slice of homemade sweet potato cheesecake - his favorite - sat on the marble island in the kitchen's center. A fork sat next to the pie. Mali always knew how to make Ezekiel feel good and he knew she was upstairs in their bedroom, waiting to make him feel even better.

Ezekiel quickly devoured the cheesecake and then sprinted upstairs to the bedroom.

Mali sat upon the bed, smiling seductively. She wore white silk lingerie and white cowry shells in her locks, which fell past her bronze shoulders.

"Blacknificent!" Ezekiel sighed as he ran his tongue slowly across his upper lip.

Mali laughed. "Blacknificent, huh? You have about a million of those, don't you?"

"Blacksolutely," Ezekiel said, smiling.

Mali extended her hands toward him. "Come here."

Ezekiel climbed into bed and embraced his wife. His body immediately relaxed and he rested his head upon her full breasts.

He examined his wife's face. Even her sightless eyes were attractive to him. "You grow more beautiful with each passing day."

Mali blushed. "Hmm…you're being awfully charming. You must *want* something. What is it, Ezekiel?"

"Only for you to say yes," Ezekiel replied.

"Yes, to what?"

Ezekiel sat up, cross-legged, on the bed and placed his hands on Mali's shoulders. "To us leaving here for a while. Taking an extended vacation."

Mali ran her soft fingertips across Ezekiel's face, examining his expression to see if he was serious. He was. "I'd love to, but work keeps you so busy, I…"

"I'm retiring tomorrow," Ezekiel chimed in. "I already sent Sweet's administrative assistant an email about it."

Mali kissed Ezekiel excitedly on the lips. "Oh, baby, that's great news! Now, I won't be up all night, worrying about you doing...whatever it is you did for Danny Sweet!"

"I know it's been hard, baby," Ezekiel said, running his fingers through Mali's locks. "But I give you my word...I'm out. It's time for us to really enjoy each other. Maybe raise a baby or two...or three."

Mali slowly pulled the straps of her lingerie top from her shoulders. "Why don't we start working on those babies right now?"

Ezekiel planted a soft kiss on Mali's neck. Her skin was sweet and soft, and he longed to explore the rest of her with his lips. "You read my mind."

CHAPTER THREE

Sweet South Records – the second wealthiest music distributor in the world – bred, born, and baptized in blood.

Formed thirty-nine years ago by a twenty-five year old drug dealer and gangbanger known as 'Sweet' Danny Sweet on the streets of Atlanta.

At fifty years of age, Sweet – as brilliant and charismatic as he was brutal and cunning – had won the support by influence, favor, or force, of nearly every black-owned record label in the United States in forming a powerful conglomerate that would control the distribution of hip-hop music.

The former powers that be in the music industry tried to stop Danny Sweet's movement, but they were ill-prepared for war with a man who not only was not afraid to do battle, but welcomed and relished it.

Those former powers were ill-prepared for the human weapons at Sweet's disposal. Weapons forged in the fires of Iraq, Cambodia, the Congo, and the cruel streets of Chicago, New York, Los Angeles, and Atlanta.

Most deadly among these weapons – Sweet's weapon of mass destruction – was a man who he had taken as a boy and had trained by the best in the ways of murder, combat tactics, stealth, and anarchy. This weapon – Ezekiel Cross – was now heading to the offices of Danny Sweet for what he hoped would be the final meeting with his mentor.

The elevator ride seemed to go on forever. Sweet loved to work in the clouds; to look down at his city and imagine himself a god, with control over the lives of the mere mortals below who worshipped and adored him.

Ezekiel hated much about Danny Sweet, but he hated Sweet's megalomania the most. Ezekiel hated his boss – the man who made him a murderer; a monster – but he remained loyal to Sweet and to The Family because they had looked out for him since he was a boy.

At the twenty-fourth floor, the elevator came to a smooth stop and the doors slid open.

Ezekiel strode out into the chic reception area of 'Sweet' Danny Sweet's office.

With a strong penchant for the color white, he had designed his office to reflect his inclination – white light reflected off of the alabaster marble floor. Ezekiel approached Corinne, Sweet's administrative assistant, who sat behind a desk of hand-carved ivory.

She smiled warmly. Her creamy skin almost matching her eggshell business suit. Such was Sweet's color obsession that he had hired Corinne more for her albinism than for her secretarial and administrative skills.

"Good morning, Mr. Cross," Corinne said. "Mr. Sweet is waiting for you. Go right on in."

"Thanks, Corinne," Ezekiel said, walking to a silver door behind her desk.

Ezekiel walked through the door and came face-to-chest with an obsidian monolith – 'Nigerian Norm'.

Norm – the Cockney, Cambridge, and Oxford-educated master-killer; a giant, whose strength matched his skill. Sweet's Chief of Security and Ezekiel's primary teacher in the traditions of dealing death – stood before Ezekiel.

The onyx giant stared Ezekiel down. His eyes pierced his student, soiling Ezekiel's soul with his fierce and unyielding gaze.

"Ezekiel," Norm said with a nod.

Ezekiel knew the drill. He raised his arms out to the side, shoulder height, and widened his stance. Norm quickly patted him down. Satisfied that Ezekiel was unarmed and not wearing a wire, Norm stepped aside, allowing Ezekiel access to yet another silver door. He stepped through the doorway into the private office of 'Sweet' Danny Sweet.

Platinum records lined the four alabaster walls – testaments to the talent of Sweet South Records' artists and to the genius of Danny Sweet.

Sweet sat in his white leather swivel chair, chewing on a stick of coconut-flavored licorice candy. His white shark skin suit and impeccable grooming belied Sweet's street-toughness and cutthroat intellect.

Ezekiel approached Sweet's desk. The music mogul rose from his chair and gave a warm hug.

"Ezekiel! Good to see you!" Sweet said happily.

"Good to be seen, Sweet," Ezekiel replied. "You have something for me?"

Sweet laughed as he returned to the comfort of his chair. "Always about the business, huh, Akin? You have to learn to lighten up, son."

"I'll keep that in mind," Ezekiel replied.

"Okay, let's get down to business, then," Sweet began.

"First, what's this I hear about you retiring?" Sweet leaned back in his chair and studied Ezekiel's face. "Corinne said something about an email? You know I don't fuck around with that technological gobbledy-goop."

"Email's been around for over forty years, Sweet, but yeah, I'm done doing wet-work."

"When were you gonna tell me?" Sweet asked, smiling.

"I just did."

Sweet snickered and nodded his shiny bald head. "Yeah, I guess you did. But, why retire? The money's good and killing's all you know how to do."

"I've been saving most of my money," Ezekiel replied. "I'm gonna invest in a few businesses…give Mali that baby she's always wanted."

Sweet's eyes widened and he shook his head in disbelief. "Baby? Aren't you afraid the kid'll catch Polio and go blind like its mama, or something?"

"Sweet, you know Mali doesn't have Polio! She went blind after suffering a head injury in an accident."

"Oh, yeah," Sweet said, snapping his fingers. "I remember vaguely. Her ex pushed her in front of a car, or some shit, right? Left *you* to pick up the pieces. You ever kill that nigga?"

"Nah, I was *fifteen*, Sweet."

"Hell, that's around the age you started merkin' motherfuckers anyway, right?"

"Something like that," Ezekiel replied.

"Well, if you need any assistance from me, let me know," Sweet said, offering Ezekiel a piece of coconut licorice.

Ezekiel waved the candy away.

"I just need you to take care of something before you run off making little Ezekiel's and shit," Sweet chuckled. "It's an easy job, but the client is offering two-hundred stacks to get it done. I won't even take my usual thirty-percent off the top…I'll just take ten. Consider it a retirement gift."

"Thanks, Sweet," Ezekiel replied. "I appreciate that."

Sweet bit into a piece of licorice, took a few quick chews and swallowed. "No problem. You've always been like a son to me, Ezekiel."

Sweet smiled slyly at his adopted son. "So, how's that beautiful mother of yours?"

"Still beautiful."

"I always had a crush on her. Your old man and I used to compete for her attention back in middle school. Obviously, *he* won."

A mask of sadness fell over

Sweet's cheerful countenance. "Caleb Cross was a hell of a man. I miss him."

"Me too," Ezekiel replied. "So, who's the mark?"

Sweet grabbed a manila folder from his desk and then slid it to Ezekiel.

Ezekiel opened the folder and studied its contents.

"Her name is Roxanne Klein," Sweet said. "She's a biophysicist. My client wants the bitch taken care of tonight. She'll be at her lab until eleven, and then she heads home."

"Consider it done."

CHAPTER FOUR

"I have a bad feeling about this, Ezekiel!"

Mali interlaced her thin fingers with her husband's and pulled him closer to her and away from his Range Rover. "Why does Sweet have to hand you your check in person? And at ten o'clock at night, to boot?"

"Baby, I don't know," Ezekiel sighed, shrugging. "Maybe Sweet is throwing me a surprise going away party."

"Okay, then I'll go with you!"

"No," Ezekiel shouted, frustrated with his failure to tell a feasible lie. "Just relax, Mali. I'll be back home in two hours, tops. Trust me."

"I *do* trust you, Ezekiel," Mali replied. "I don't trust *Sweet*!"

She released her husband's hand.

Ezekiel kissed Mali's forehead and then hopped in the Range Rover. "See you soon, love."

Mali waved goodbye and then wrapped her arms around her chest as if to hold in her fear, lest it burst forth and consume her.

Ezekiel pulled out of the garage, down the driveway and into the street. He peered into his rearview mirror and took a long look at his wife before he sped off into the muggy Atlanta night.

CHAPTER FIVE

The street was quiet.

Ezekiel thanked God for sound dampening technology - not one note of music escaped the Range Rover's interior as Ezekiel calmed his nerves to the haunting lamentations of Eddie Hazel's lead guitar in Funkadelic's 'Maggot Brain'.

"Nearly seventy years old and you're *still* hot," Ezekiel whispered to the song.

As the music faded, he

forcefully racked the slide of his pistol, slamming a round into the chamber.

The assassin slid out of his vehicle and assessed his surroundings. Satisfied that no one was watching, Ezekiel sprinted toward the largest warehouse, at the end of the cul-de-sac.

His movement was swift...silent.

He found himself thanking God again – this time, for Chagga Mutwa, patriarch of the Tokoloshe guild of assassins and expert in the arts of invisibility and quiescence.

Ezekiel had spent two years of harsh training, at the foot of Mount Kilimanjaro, under the tutelage of the sapient old master.

In those two years, he had learned much.

Ezekiel tested the front door. The steel entryway creaked

open. No surprise. Engineers'
Row - or, 'The Twilight Zone', as
the youth called it - was
patrolled and protected by
fearsome and efficient nano-
drones.

Swarming an intruder by the
thousands, these nearly
microscopic, cybernetic organisms
invaded a victim's body through
his orifices. The minuscule
drones would then connect to the
victim's nervous system and shut
the intruder down, rendering him
comatose until the arrival of the
police.

Of course, when your boss is
Danny Sweet - owner of the company
that created the drones - the
little terrors presented no
problem at all.

Ezekiel crept into the
warehouse. Through the dim light,
he could see rows of crates filled
with wires, computer parts,
electronic gadgets, rods, gears,
and motors of various sizes. The
hangar-sized warehouse reeked with

the smell of copper and axle grease.

Suddenly, voices came – low and in a staccato rhythm. Ezekiel crouched low and tilted his head toward the sound. No, not voices, Ezekiel realized. A single voice. A woman's voice…rapping a tune from his early childhood.

His father would play the song and talk about the rapper performing it as if the man was a god. "Biggie is a genius!" his father would proclaim. "The mad scientist of hip-hop!"

The name of the song came to Ezekiel – 'Warning'.

The assassin moved across the warehouse in a quick, zigzagging shuffle.

The woman's voice grew louder.

"…*I got the Calico with the black talons loaded in the clip.*"

The voice was coming from a

small office at the rear of the warehouse. Ezekiel rushed toward the office door, aimed his pistol and snatched the door wide open.

He rolled into the room, quickly popping up to a kneeling position, with his pistol at the ready.

The room, however, was empty, save a large plasma television in the corner of the room. On top of the television sat what appeared to be a gold watch.

Suddenly, the door slammed shut. Ezekiel whirled around to face it.

The low click that followed told him that the door had locked.

Ezekiel aimed his pistol at the doorknob.

The television came to life with a soft hum. *"I wouldn't do that if I was you."*

Ezekiel turned toward the television. On the screen was a

smiling woman, whose wrinkled brow and sagging jowls set her age around sixty. The puffs under her blue eyes and her pale skin told Ezekiel that the woman spent most of her days indoors. He recognized the woman from her dossier – Dr. Roxanne Klein.

"There are odorless, invisible gasses in this room," Dr. Klein said. "Quite *volatile* gasses. If you fire that weapon, you'll die."

"What in the hell is going on?" Ezekiel inquired.

"A little…experiment," Dr. Klein responded. "A *big* experiment, actually."

Dr. Klein looked from side to side and then leaned closer to the camera, her face filling the entire television screen. She whispered as if others could hear them. "We – my friend – are about to make history!"

"*We* aren't about to do a

damned thing," Ezekiel replied. "*You* are going to die if you don't let me out of here right now!"

"If I let you out, you're going to kill me anyway," Dr. Klein said, wagging her index finger at Ezekiel. "That – after all – is what we hired you to do."

Ezekiel's eyes diminished to slivers and the right corner of his top lip turned upward. His face, now, a mask of confusion, he replied – "We?"

"Yes, your boss – Mr. Sweet – and I."

"Danny Sweet set *me* up?"

"He said you were retiring," Dr. Klein replied. "I guess murderers like you don't get gold watches...you get...on second thought, you *do* get a gold watch. If you look..."

"So," Ezekiel said, interrupting her. "Sweet sends an old, ugly ass scientist broad to kill me? Doesn't make sense."

Dr. Klein's eyes widened in shock. "Kill you? Oh, no, my boy," she said, shaking her head. The silver-gray bun at the crest of it oscillated like a bobble head toy. "You are too valuable for that – which is why I forgive your disparaging comment about my backside."

"I was referring to your face."

Dr. Klein's smile faded. "Oh."

She paused for a moment, seeming to reassess Ezekiel's insult and then her smile returned. "Mr. Sweet has invested heavily in the creation that you are standing in – the culmination of thirty years of research."

"An empty room?" Ezekiel asked. "Sweet needs to fire his financial advisors."

"A room, yes, but I assure you, it is not empty," Dr. Klein replied. "There are things within

the walls…the floor…the ceiling –
that you could not imagine!"

Dr. Klein closed her eyes,
took a deep breath and sighed
softly. Her smile widened. "You
– my friend – are standing in the
first and only…fully
operational…temporal displacement
chamber!"

Ezekiel stared at the
television screen. His expression
was blank. "Temporal displace…a
friggin' time machine?"

Laughter erupted from
Ezekiel's chest and exploded from
his chest. "Lady, let me out of
here so I can hurry up and kill
you and then take care of Sweet's
treacherous ass!"

Dr. Klein shook her head. "I
guess I'll just have to show you."

The biophysicist tilted her
camera downward. Ezekiel could
see a panel, with a series of
buttons and levers. A laptop
computer sat in Dr. Klein's lap.

The scientist began turning dials and pulling levers and then she typed something on her laptop's keyboard. "I will be sending you twenty-seven years into the past. Anything I have sent beyond that has…well, let's just say my pet chimp, Rocky, has seen better days."

Dr. Klein returned the camera to her face. She pointed upward, following her forefinger with her eyes toward the top of the screen. "Now, if you look on top of this television, you will see a watch."

Ezekiel approached the television cautiously. The watch was gold, with a platinum bezel and hands. Ezekiel picked up the watch and weighed it in his hands. It was heavier than a normal watch of its size and was of a masterful craftsmanship.

"The watch is actually a tracking device that will allow me to monitor your place in time. If you wear it, I can also monitor your vital signs."

Ezekiel slipped the watch into his jacket pocket.

"If you survive the temporal displacement," Dr. Klein continued. "I promise I'll bring you back to our present…*after* I have ensured that I am far from here and safe from you."

"You promise? How nice of you?" Ezekiel spat.

"I can't win the Nobel Prize without my test subject as evidence my invention works, now can I?" Dr. Klein responded. "Mr. Sweet even guarantees he'll let you live when you return. Of course, he'll be keeping your mother and your wife as insurance that you won't come after him."

"You send me *any*where," Ezekiel began, clutching his fists in anger. "And I promise you, I will find you and kill you in the past so none of this ever happened!"

Dr. Klein laughed. "Ah, the

old 'Grandfather Paradox'. It won't happen. Paradox doesn't exist. See, physicists are trying to send the physical body back in time, but flesh, blood and bone cannot survive the journey."

Dr. Klein placed her fingertips upon the top of her head and massaged her scalp. "It is the *mind* that I send back. It is the mind that returns."

"And what of the body?" Ezekiel asked. "What happens to it?"

"Physics does not allow the body to travel through time. However, the mind is not subject to the laws of physics."

"So, my body dies."

"Disintegrates. The mind – which moves at twenty four billion miles per second – almost instantaneously recreates the body from the disintegrated particles."

"You're insane."

"Did you know that primates raised around humans see themselves as human?" Dr Klein asked, ignoring him. "Rocky…he thought he was human. On his first temporal displacement – I sent him back ninety-six seconds – I brought him back and received quite a shock. Rocky returned as a well-formed teenaged male *human*."

Dr. Klein scratched the top of her head and poked out her lower jaw, mimicking the gestures of an ape. "Rocky's behavior and activities were still those of a chimpanzee – albeit a domesticated one."

Dr. Klein tapped her temple with her fingers. "It was his *mind*, you see? Whatever your self-image - upon reintegration after temporal displacement – *that* is how you recreate yourself."

"So, a ninety pound anorexic would recreate herself as a morbidly obese fat ass," Ezekiel said.

"Yes."

"You are crazy as a shit-house rat," Ezekiel replied, shaking his head. "Let me out of this room now!"

"Sorry. No can do," Dr. Klein said. "You are about to *make* history…or *become* it!"

"Klein, you're dead," Ezekiel shouted. "You hear me? Dead!"

The assassin's ears were suddenly assaulted by a deafening buzz. He felt as if his nerves had been wrapped in barbed wire and rusty nails were being driven into his skull. His teeth shifted in his mouth and then collapsed, sideways, upon each other, like dominoes.

Ezekiel dropped his revolver and collapsed to his knees, screaming and clutching the sides of his head, as if trying to keep his mind from seeping through the fissures in his swiftly unraveling brain.

And then the room was engulfed in intense and total blinding...white...light.

CHAPTER SIX

The buzzing stopped.

Ezekiel's very being – just moments before, torn asunder – slammed back together, as his mind summoned his scattered molecules and stitched them together in their familiar pattern.

A sudden maelstrom of nausea dropped him to his knees. The maelstrom whirled and frothed in his gut and then rose – as a tsunami – to his throat.

Wave after wave of vomit

erupted from Ezekiel's mouth, nose, and the corners of his eyes.

Through a billowing haze of dizziness and disorientation, a soft, pale, blue light shined. Ezekiel crawled to it, his body shivering from the cold concrete floor's hard caress upon his nakedness.

The light began to fade. Ezekiel reached out to it and his hands fell upon something small…metal…"The watch," he gasped.

Dr. Klein had designed the thing to withstand what his body could not – a three-decade journey through time and space.

Ezekiel clutched the watch and then pressed his fist to his chest, trying to synchronize the erratic beating of his heart with the steady *tick*, *tick*, *tick* of the second hand.

The dizziness subsided, but the cold that nipped at his naked flesh did not. Ezekiel hid his hands under his forearms and rubbed his sinewy arms up and down his chest.

With the warmth slowly returning to his limbs, Ezekiel walked on wobbly legs toward the door.

Suddenly, it flung open. The stench of crack cocaine, sweat, and feces rushed in.

Besieged by the malodorous assault, Ezekiel could no longer fight his nausea and vomit burst forth once again. Dizziness dropped him to his knees.

Three intruders – two men and one woman – barged into the room.

The largest man – tall and lean – probably an athlete before drug abuse overcame him – drove a filthy, sandaled foot into Ezekiel's jaw, sending him sliding backward.

Ezekiel rolled to his feet – by instinct more than by will –

and assumed a fighting stance, crouching low and arching his back like a cat about to pounce on its prey.

The tall man charged. His shorter, pudgy friend followed closely behind.

Ezekiel exploded forward, driving his left knee into the tall man's gut.

The man fell to the ground, screaming and twitching from the agony of a ruptured liver.

Dizziness struck again. Ezekiel stumbled backward a few steps and fell flat on his back.

The other male knelt beside him and pressed something hard and metallic against his skull.

The man's pudgy gut flopped against Ezekiel's face. The brown, tweed jacket that covered the man's rotund belly reeked of body fluids and cheap cologne.

Ezekiel's waves of nausea

grew more turbulent.

The pudgy man tilted his head back slightly and looked down his nose at Ezekiel's face. "This, my good man, is a robbery," he began. "My name is Chuck Alexander Etheridge…"

"Shakespeare!" the woman giggled.

"Don't be a boor," Shakespeare said. "Yes, the denizens of this metropolis have, indeed, dubbed me Shakespeare."

The woman caressed Ezekiel's muscular thighs. Her dirty fingernails traced pale-gray lines on his dark skin. She licked her lips lewdly as she stared at his sizable member.

"And the lascivious creature between your loins is Janine," Shakespeare said.

"Put that gun away now and I'll let you both live," Ezekiel said.

"Give us what you hidin' in yo' hand and we out," Janine replied. "Tryin' to be slick, huh?"

Janine snatched the watch from Ezekiel's fist and handed it to Shakespeare.

"He didn't realize that he's dealing with professionals," Shakespeare said. "My friend, we have been…"

Ezekiel struck lightning fast. He twisted Shakespeare's wrist in a painful joint-lock and then snatched the pistol from the pudgy man's weakened grasp.

Ezekiel fired.

Janine screamed as a bullet tore into her thigh.

She buckled forward, screaming as she collapsed onto her chest.

Shakespeare leaped to his feet and dashed toward the door. "Please, don't shoot me! I'm sorry! I'm sorry!"

Ezekiel crawled toward the tall man, who had fallen unconscious from pain. "This fool's funky clothes will have to do for now," Ezekiel whispered.

And then – out of the disorientation of being ripped apart and put back together; through the haze of dizziness still hovering over him - it came to him.

"The *watch*! Damn!"

Ezekiel forced himself back to his feet and ran out of the office. He quickly assessed his surroundings. The only thing in the wide open space of the warehouse was a thick film of dust.

Ezekiel shambled toward the exit, battling the raging nausea and dizziness that now felt like forces of nature. He threw his body against the door and it swung open. The cold night air cleared his head...enough to hear the roar of the engine...enough to see the lights speeding toward him...but not enough to avoid them.

He summoned enough will to throw his body upward, onto the hood of the car and roll with the impact.

Ezekiel slid off the hood and struck the ground hard. He rolled a few feet and then came to rest, sprawled on the pavement.

He struggled to open his eyes, but it felt as if weights were sewed to each eyelash.

He tried to scream, but his lips remained firmly pressed together.

Thankfully, he could still hear.

"Oh, my god!" a woman's voice shouted. Her voice was rich, soothing...and oddly familiar. "Is he okay? Did you hit him?"

"I...I think so," a man's voice

– also, strangely familiar – answered. The man's voice was shaky – filled with concern – but there was no fear in it. "No…I…maybe. I don't know."

"Sir?" the woman asked. Fear *was* in *her* voice.

"Sir are you okay?" the man repeated. "Sir?!"

The world began to spin rapidly and the voices faded into darkness.

Spinning.   Darkness.

Spinning.   Darkness.

Spinning.

Darkness.

Spin.

Dark.

Spin.

CHAPTER SEVEN

Ezekiel's skin was moist and cool.

Dr. Nora Mitchell examined the bruises and abrasions that polka-dotted his body.

Dr. Mitchell snatched a fistful of gauze pads from her bag and placed them on the nightstand. She reached into her bag again and extracted two bottles – one, a small bottle of iodine; the other, a large bottle of saline.

The door to the room opened

and a man with strong, handsome features poked his head inside. "How is he, Doc?"

Dr. Mitchell waved the man inside and then she gently sat on the bed next to Ezekiel. "He has a minor concussion and a score of bruises and abrasions."

Dr. Mitchell pointed to the mound of pillows on both sides of Ezekiel's head. "I am trying to stabilize his head as much as possible."

"Is his neck broken?" a woman asked as she entered the room.

"No," Dr. Mitchell replied. "The endolymph in his ear – the fluids that control equilibrium – are sloshing around out of control. I've never seen anything like it."

"Is he going to be okay?" the woman asked.

"I believe so," Dr. Mitchell answered. "But, this man should have been taken to a hospital,

Lydia. If his condition worsens, you and Caleb are going to have a big problem."

"I hit him, Doc," Caleb said. "You know I can't bring any heat from the police down on me. Sweet would have my head."

"I know," Dr. Mitchell replied. "We all have to keep Sweet happy."

Lydia waved her hand, as if shooing flies, and rolled her eyes. "Oh, please."

"Come on, Lydia," Caleb sighed. "Give Sweet a break."

Lydia rolled her eyes again and folded her arms against her chest.

Caleb withdrew his wallet from the back pocket of his jeans. "How much do we owe you, Doc?"

"Nothing," Dr. Mitchell replied. "I still owe *you* for helping out Dee-Dee."

"I just put her demo in Sweet's hands," Caleb said. "Your baby's talent sold it. That girl can *sang*!"

Dr. Mitchell zipped her bag and tossed its strap over her shoulder. "Still, you opened the door."

"Consider us even, then," Caleb replied.

"Well, I'm going to take my leave now," Dr. Mitchell said. "Lydia, wash his wounds with the saline and apply the iodine, then cover the wounds in gauze. Call me if you have questions."

"Okay, we will," Lydia replied.

"Let me walk you to the door," Caleb said.

The trio exited the room, closing the door behind them.

Ezekiel remained in dreamless slumber, in a whirling world of eternal night.

CHAPTER EIGHT

The world came to a screeching halt and darkness gave way to light. Ezekiel studied his surroundings. The red oak ceiling fan...the navy curtains...the chest with the small plasma television...all familiar somehow.

The bed he lay in...the lemony smell of the bed-sheets and the shadows in the corners of the room...all *too* familiar.

Fear uncoiled in his belly and slithered up his spine. Ezekiel's heart threatened to burst from his chest. "Impossible," he whispered.

Ezekiel had not felt fear in nearly three decades and he allowed it to take him for a while before quelling it with his breathing as he had been taught long ago.

The door opened and Caleb walked in, smiling and carrying a glass of water.

Ezekiel jumped backward, slamming his back into the headboard.

"Easy," Caleb said softly. "Easy. I'm Caleb Cross. This is my home. What's your name?"

Ezekiel felt dizzy. Not from fluids swirling around in his cranium, but from the shock of staring into his father's face. A man who died when Ezekiel was just fifteen years old.

"My name? Oh…umm…Jason…Jason Locke," he lied. "I'll be damned! This is my…how?"

"Huh?" Caleb replied.

"Nothing," Ezekiel said. "I'm still a little…disoriented."

Caleb handed the water to Ezekiel. "My wife and I brought you here after I struck you with our car."

"Struck me?"

"You were naked and in a daze; ran right out in front of us."

"I vaguely remember that"

"Question, Mr. Locke…"

"Please," Ezekiel said. "Call me Jason."

"Alright, Jason," Caleb replied. "You were naked as a jaybird, chasing God-knows-who, and strapped with a forty-five. You a cop with a freaky side, or are you 'Mister Raper-Man'?"

"Neither," Ezekiel said. "I was wasted. Some guys offered me a ride home. They took me to that warehouse you saw me run out of."

Ezekiel studied Caleb's face to see if he had discerned the lie. He had not.

"They robbed me," Ezekiel continued. "They took my clothes; my money; my...oh, shit, my watch!" Ezekiel pounded a fist into the mattress.

"What about it? Was it expensive, or something? Important to you?" Caleb asked.

"The most important thing in the *world* right now! A retirement gift."

"And the gun? Was that a retirement gift too?"

"I took it from one of the guys when he was distracted," Ezekiel replied. "They hauled ass. I followed."

"So, where did you retire from?" Caleb asked. "What kind of work did you do?"

"I arranged funerals."

"Were you good at it?"

"The best."

"Well, I'm in security myself," Caleb said. "I'm a bodyguard, actually, and a retired Marine Corps sniper."

"I know," Ezekiel replied. He took a sip of water. It felt soothing to his throat and cooled his insides. He took another sip.

"You know?" Caleb asked.

Ezekiel nearly choked on his water. "I mean…I can tell you're former military. You have that demeanor about you."

"Yeah, once a Marine, always a Marine."

"*Ah, I see our guest is awake.*"

Ezekiel snapped his head toward the voice. That rich alto, which soothed him as a child, scolded him, comforted him all his

60

life.

"Hey, baby," Caleb said, looking back, over his shoulder. "Jason, this is my wife, Lydia; Lydia, this is Mr. Jason Locke."

Lydia reached out her hand. Ezekiel's fingers shook as he touched his mother's flesh. His mother who - at this moment - was younger than him. The dizziness slowly crept back in and the world tilted a little.

"Pleased to meet you, Jason," Lydia said, smiling warmly.

Lydia pulled someone into the room. Ezekiel's heart began to race and the world rocked back and forth.

"And this is our son, Ezekiel," Lydia said, pulling a tall, lanky young man into view. "But everyone calls him 'Z'."

The world turned upside down and - once again - Ezekiel succumbed to the darkness.

CHAPTER NINE

The smell of grilled meat awakened him. The rumblings in Ezekiel's stomach reminded him that he had not eaten in days.

He slowly rose from his bed and waited. The dizziness he expected did not come. Ezekiel grabbed the rash-guard shirt and the surfers' board-shorts – which were folded neatly at the foot of the bed – and shambled to the bathroom. He looked forward to washing his wounds and massaging his aching muscles in the shower.

The warm water cleared his head. Ezekiel stepped out of the shower and inspected his body. The bruises were no longer visible and the abrasions were healing well.

After getting dressed, Ezekiel followed his nose to the dining room downstairs.

Lydia, Caleb, and Z sat at the dining table, eating grilled chicken and baked potatoes - Caleb's favorite.

Lydia spotted Ezekiel first. "Good afternoon, Jason!"

"Good afternoon," Ezekiel replied.

"Come join us, Jason," Caleb said. "You hungry?"

"Hungry enough to eat a bear!" Ezekiel replied.

The dining room exploded with laughter.

Ezekiel's eyes darted from

face to face, searching for the source of his hosts' merriment. "It wasn't that funny…"

"My dad always says the same thing," Z replied.

"Oh. Strange coincidence, I guess," Ezekiel said.

The assassin sat next to Z. Doing so felt surreal and Ezekiel fought the urge to stare at his younger self.

Lydia handed Ezekiel a plate of food, which he did not hesitate to tear into. When he finally looked up from the delicious – and long overdue – meal, he noticed Lydia staring at him. "Is something wrong?" he asked.

"No," Lydia began. "I'm sorry. Please, forgive me for staring, but God, you look just like my uncle, Steve!"

"They say we all have a twin somewhere," Ezekiel replied.

Ezekiel looked at Z, who was

busy devouring a chicken breast, which he had drowned in barbecue sauce. Ezekiel smiled. He still loved his chicken that way. "How are *you* doing, little brother?"

Z wiped his mouth with a napkin. The chicken remained in one hand. "I'm good! So, how long are you gonna be staying in my room, Mr. Locke?"

"Z!" Lydia shouted, tossing a piece of baked potato at his head.

Without looking, the young man plucked the piece of potato out of the air and then ate it.

"Don't be rude to our guest, son!" Caleb ordered.

"It's okay," Ezekiel replied. "I won't be putting you out much longer, Z. I feel a lot better now."

Ezekiel turned his attention to the head of the table. "Thanks for the clothes, Caleb."

"No problem," Caleb said. "Just some old stuff from my mixed martial arts days."

"Dad was Regional Champion in MMA!" Z said.

"Caleb was convinced he was going to be the next star of that 'Ultimate Fighting' show that comes on TV," Lydia said, giggling.

"They called me to be on the show," Caleb replied. "But they wanted me for the middleweight season. I'm six-four, two-hundred fifty-pounds, there is no way in hell I was going to cut over sixty pounds for a damned television show."

"So, where do you live, Jason?" Lydia asked.

"I actually just got into town," Jason replied. "I'll be staying at a motel until I find an apartment."

Caleb and Lydia looked at each other. Caleb raised his

eyebrows and cut his eyes at Ezekiel. Lydia nodded.

"Look, Jason," Caleb began. "Lydia and I have been looking for someone to rent our basement apartment. It's spacious, furnished, and clean."

"Our former tenant got married and moved out a couple of months ago," Lydia chimed in.

"If you take the spot, you'll have your own entrance," Caleb said. "Rent's only five-hundred a month. Utilities are on us, but you'll have to get your own phone."

Ezekiel smiled and shook his head. "Thanks, you are both too kind, but I couldn't."

"Well, we could use the extra money, to be honest," Lydia replied.

"Yeah, times are a bit harder since I retired from the military," Caleb said. "If it wasn't for Lydia teaching, we'd *really* be in jam."

"Doesn't bodyguard work pay pretty well?" Ezekiel asked.

Caleb placed a heavy hand on Z's shoulder. Z closed his eyes and shook his head. He knew what was coming.

"Son, step out for a minute," Caleb said. "You can take your plate with you."

"Aw, Dad, come on," Z said, rolling his eyes. "Why do I have to leave? I'm fifteen, not five!"

"Ezekiel Cross!" Lydia shouted. "Do what your father told you to do!"

Z rose from the table, grabbed his plate and hung his head. "Yes, ma'am," he sighed, as he shuffled out of the room.

"I work for Danny Sweet," Caleb said. "CEO of Sweet South Records. Ever heard of him?"

"Of course," Ezekiel replied.

"He owns one of the most successful record distribution companies in the world."

"Who told you *that* lie?" Caleb snickered. "Sweet South is a record *label* – it doesn't distribute – but Sweet *is* working on something big that he believes will change the music industry forever."

"My gut tells me he'll succeed in a few years," Ezekiel said.

"I hope so," Caleb replied. "Maybe then, he'll pay me more."

"I doubt it," Lydia said, shaking her head.

Caleb rolled his eyes. "See, Danny Sweet, Lydia, and I grew up together. When I found myself in a financial bind after I was discharged from the Marines, Sweet hired me as one of his bodyguards. The pay is crappy, though."

"What?" Ezekiel said, shocked. "As much money as Sweet

makes?"

"He only hired Caleb to flaunt his riches over him," Lydia said.

"Come on, Lydia," Caleb sighed. "I just don't believe that."

Lydia tossed her fork onto her plate and leered at her husband. "Open your eyes, Caleb! Danny has always wanted me; since we were kids. Baby, when you and I got involved, he felt like you beat him. He's always wanted to get back at you for that."

"Well, I hope you're wrong," Caleb replied. "Anyway, what do you say about our apartment, Jason?"

"If it will help you guys out…okay."

"Good," Caleb said, smiling broadly. "You need any help moving your stuff out of storage?"

"No, I actually decided to

start fresh when I moved here," Ezekiel answered. "I'll have the five-hundred dollars by tonight."

Caleb stood and then extended his hand. Ezekiel stood, took his father's hand in his and shook it.

"Welcome home, Jason," Caleb said.

"Home," Ezekiel echoed. "I'm home."

CHAPTER TEN

The old neighborhood was as spirited as Ezekiel remembered it.

Old men sat on porches and on the hoods of cars, sharing forty-ounce bottles of malt liquor and swapping hyperbolized tales of days gone by.

Young women sat on steps, braiding and twisting their daughters', nieces', and boyfriends' hair.

And on the corner - looming and ever-present - were the peddlers of powdered death; the white-rock Reapers.

Lord among them was Danny Sweet's street Lieutenant,

Frankie, and his Chief Enforcers, 'Morocco' and 'Head'.

Ezekiel moved like a specter, appearing in one shadow, disappearing, and appearing in another. As always, he thanked God for the masters who taught him how to move, to be silent, to be unseen, to kill. He whispered their names with great honor and reverence – "Chagga Mutwa, Norman Uti, Colonel Thomas Fu-Kiau."

From the darkness, Ezekiel observed Frankie and his men serve the lengthy procession of dead-eyed, cadaverous crack-addicts. A row of strategically placed trees obscured the operation from unwanted eyes.

A pudgy man in a dingy, gray, wool suit strolled to the front of the line.

"Shakespeare," Ezekiel whispered.

Shakespeare stood before Frankie with his chest thrust

forward, chin slightly raised, and a smug smile.

"Fuck you smilin' fo', shawty?" Frankie growled. "What you want? And if you ask fo' a rock on credit, I'm a slap the shit out you!"

Shakespeare continued to smile as he thrust a gold and platinum watch in Frankie's face.

Ezekiel's whole body tensed and he fought back the urge to charge the man. "Damn! The watch!"

"I'll take two rocks, please," Shakespeare said.

Frankie pushed his chest out until his back formed a deep bow. He thrust his shoulders back and raised his chin until he was looking skyward. "I'll take two rocks, please," he said, nearly perfectly mimicking Shakespeare's voice.

Head, Morocco, and the queue of crack-heads laughed.

Shakespeare's eyes flitted erratically and his caramel skin reddened. Sweat formed on his brow and ran down his nose.

"Nigga think he at the Ritz, don't he?" Frankie snickered.

More laughter.

"P-Please, just take the watch," Shakespeare sighed. "It is very valuable. A family heirloom. Please, take it and give me my merchandise, sir."

Frankie snatched the watch from Shakespeare's fat fingers and examined it.

Morocco reached into the pocket of his denim jacket and withdrew two tiny, off-white rocks, which were wrapped in plastic. He handed the dope to Head, who then approached Shakespeare.

Frankie thrust out his arm sideways and placed his palm upon Head's chest, stopping the enforcer in his tracks.

"Hold up, playboy," Frankie said.

Frankie looked up from the watch and stared Shakespeare down. "You playin' games with me, shawty?"

"Games? What? No!" Shakespeare cried. "However, I do rather enjoy a nice round of cricket, perhaps…"

"Cricket?" Frankie interrupted. "Do I look like Harry Porter to you, shawty?"

"No, no…that's *Potter*…and the game you refer to is Quid…"

The back-hand slap rang out. Shakespeare stumbled backward, holding his jaw.

The line of crack-heads dispersed. Violence at a crack-spot meant no service for a few hours as things were allowed to cool down and alibis were formed.

Zombie-fiends shambled off into the night, murmuring their

protest.

"How you gon' try to give me a watch that runs backward, shawty?" Frankie said. "The hands are movin' *counter-*clockwise!"

Frankie drove his fist into Shakespeare's solar plexus. The dope-addictfell to his knees as he vomited a rush of air.

Sweet's Lieutenant struck again, delivering a powerful uppercut punch to Shakespeare's face.

His head jerked back and blood sprayed from his mouth.

Frankie snatched a baseball bat from its resting place against the fence that surrounded the corner house. He raised the bat above his head and prepared to strike.

Suddenly, the door to the house on the corner flew open.

Frankie stopped his attack

with the bat in mid-swing.

Nigerian Norm burst from the house. A beautiful, young woman, with ample endowments, followed closely behind him.

"Are you off your fuckin' rocker?" Norm shouted. "You tryin' to bring the John Hops?"

"The who?" Frankie asked with a shrug.

"The cops, you wanker!" Norm replied.

Frankie hung his head. He had seen Nigerian Norm literally break a man in half for angering him. Although he was Sweet's best worker on the streets, Frankie did not dare push Norm's buttons. "Sorry, Norm."

Norm tapped Morocco in the chest with the back of his hand, which was half as big as the enforcer's torso. Morocco staggered backward a few steps from the force of the "gentle" blow.

"Can you Adam this Brad Pitt?" Norm spat in a strong Cockney accent. "I'm in the fuckin' cat, with that fine twist – who just run off, thanks to you – and she's givin' me a heavenly on me Gregory," Norm kissed the tips of his fingers and pressed them to his neck. "When I butcher's out the window and see you in a read with a bleedin' Boutros Gali loaf!"

Frankie exchanged a quick glance with Head, who shrugged and pursed his lips sideways.

"Umm...sorry...Norm?" Frankie replied.

Norm patted himself on the forehead. "Oy, forgive *me*, mate. When I gets pissed, I resort back to me Cockney roots."Norm laughed. "You blokes have no idea what the hell I was sayin', huh?"

Norm snapped his head in Shakespeare's direction. The pudgy, little dope-head was still on his knees, holding his aching face and dabbing his bloody mouth with the sleeve of his suit coat.

"So, what's the story with the crack-head?" Norm inquired.

"He gave me this watch," Frankie said, handing the watch to Norm. "Looks good, but the hands are running counter-clockwise and shit."

"Lemme see," Norm said, examining the watch carefully. "Hello! Nice weight…gold…platinum…"

He placed the watch to his ear and smiled. "I like the oddity of the hands movin' backward…'sankofa' and all that."

The giant pointed at Head. "Give the man his merchandise!"

Head handed Shakespeare the tiny off-white rocks of crack.

The drug addict pulled himself to his feet and scurried off. "Thank you, kind sir!"

Norm held the watch up high. "I just found Sweet's birthday gift!"

The giant slipped the watch into the inner pocket of his blazer and then hopped into his Cadillac SUV. "Later, gents."

Norm sped off into the night.

Ezekiel waited a few moments and then walked briskly toward Frankie and his men.

"What up, shawty?" Frankie asked. "How can we help you?"

Ezekiel stopped a few feet from the men. He locked his gaze on Frankie. "Take out your weapons and toss them over to me."

Frankie looked over his shoulder, from Head to Morocco, who were both snickering. He then returned his attention to the man who had dared give him such a demand. "You forgot to take out *your* weapon before coming at us like this, didn't you?"

"I *am* a weapon," Ezekiel replied. "Now, toss your guns over to me, gentlemen."

"You sure you wanna do this?" Frankie asked. "Do you have any idea who you fuckin' with?"

Ezekiel took two steps toward Sweet's Lieutenant. "If I have to repeat myself, I am going to stomp your head into wine."

Frankie shook his head and spat on the ground angrily. He snapped his fingers and then thrust an index finger toward Ezekiel and spoke to his cronies, "Man, y'all hurry up, take this crazy nigga somewhere and kill him, so we can get back to business! But, keep it quiet!"

Head moved first. He quickly snatched up the baseball bat and exploded forward, swinging the Louisville Slugger in a wide arc at Ezekiel's torso.

Ezekiel darted toward Head and delivered a sharp, downward

elbow strike to the man's forearm.

The enforcer winced in pain as the punishing elbow pounded down onto pressure points in his arm. The bat fell from his suddenly numb fingers.

Ezekiel followed with a powerful head-butt to Head's chin.

Head's eyes went dead and his legs buckled. The enforcer fell - unconscious - onto his back.

A pulverizing downward knee to the throat ensured Ezekiel that Head would never again regain consciousness.

Morocco charged head first, like a raging rhinoceros.

Ezekiel leaped toward the big man and locked his arm around Morocco's neck, pressing the bone of his wrist into the enforcer's windpipe.

Morocco continued to charge forward, in hopes of escaping Ezekiel's grip, his powerful legs moving both of their muscular frames up the street.

Ezekiel squeezed Morocco's thick neck with all his might and dropped his weight down onto the big man's shoulders.

Morocco collapsed onto all fours. His legs flailed in panic as the guillotine-choke tightened around his neck and dug into his Adam's apple.

Ezekiel held the choke, cutting off the flow of blood to Morocco's brain and the air to his lungs.

The Chief Enforcer shook violently. A patch of wetness grew in his pants and a trail of urine ran down his legs, soaking his socks.

The smell of feces permeated the air. Frankie leaned against the fence and vomited; blood and guts, he was used to, but shit, piss and a man's eyes nearly popping out of his head were too much to take in.

Morocco's convulsions stopped.

Ezekiel released the enforcer and his body fell to the ground with a soft, wet thud.

Ezekiel rose and ran toward Frankie, who still leaned against the fence, retching.

Frankie's fingers fumbled at the holster on his belt. Before he could draw his gun, however, Ezekiel grabbed his wrist and twisted forcefully.

Frankie screamed as tendons and ligaments were torn apart.

Ezekiel twisted Frankie's wrist in the opposite direction, which sent the drug lord flipping through the air.

Frankie's back slammed onto the pavement and the air was instantly pulled from his lungs.

Ezekiel raised his boot high

above Frankie's face and then drove it downward, delivering a brutal stomp.

Blood sprayed from Frankie's mouth and nose.

Ezekiel followed with another hard stomp. Then another...and another...and...another.

Frankie's arms and legs spasmed erratically.

Ezekiel delivered several more stomps to the Lieutenant's head.

Frankie's face flattened to half its depth. Blood and tissue poured forth from his eyes, nose, mouth, and ears. The drug lord twitched once...again...and then, lay still.

Ezekiel ran into the house.

Less than two minutes later, he emerged from the shadowed area carrying a duffel bag, which was nearly filled to bursting with stacks of hundred dollar bills.

Ezekiel stepped into a shadow and walked, unseen, into the night.

CHAPTER ELEVEN

The man strained at the ropes, which bound his wrists and ankles. He pushed against the balled-up, blood-soaked handkerchief that was stuffed into his mouth. The chair, to which the man was strapped, rocked back and forth as he thrashed wildly.

Danny Sweet stood behind the man. His shark-skin suit was immaculately white. The duo of giants flanking him, however, was soiled with the blood of their captive.

Norm was especially bloody. No one enjoyed meting out brutality like Nigerian Norm.

Detective Terry McGraw smacked their captive on the side of the head. The thrashing stopped.

Z walked into the room. Tears had dried on his face, forming white streaks on his cheeks.

Sweet greeted Z with a smile. "What's up, little man? You ready to do this?"

"Y-yeah, I guess," Z replied.

"You guess?" Norm sneered.

The Nigerian giant drew his pistol from its holster and rammed it into Z's chest. "Take it!"

Z stood still. He fought to control his breathing and to quell his nausea.

Norm pushed the gun into Z's chest again. This time with a bit more force. "You'd better take this gun, little Rob Roy and man up!"

"Norm, please," Sweet crooned. "Please, forgive Nigerian Norm, Z. He just gets a little excited at times."

Sweet gestured toward the gun with his hand. "Go ahead, son. Take it."

Z grabbed the pistol with both hands and held it to his chest. The gun rose and fell in waves with each powerful beat of his heart.

"That's my boy," Sweet shouted. "Son, this piece of shit right here is Greg Blake – the man who took your father from you."

Greg shook his head and murmured through his gag.

"He murdered Caleb in cold blood," Sweet continued. "And for what? A few dollars?"

Sweet slithered behind Z,

laying a hand on one of the young man's shoulders and resting his chin on the other. "For that, he deserves to die, doesn't he?"

Z stared into Greg's eyes, which were wide with terror. The young man looked inward and searched his feelings. There were none, save a thirst for revenge. He nodded in agreement with Sweet. Greg Blake deserved to die.

"Then it's only fitting that *you* do it, son," Sweet said. "You're the man in the family now and you have to *show* motherfuckers that you're the man by doing man *shit*, son."

"That's right," Norm chimed in. "Punch this wanker's dickory!"

Z pointed the pistol at Greg's chest.

Greg jumped in his chair and desperately strained against his binds. Blood began to trickle from the abrasions in his wrists.

The world seemed to slow down and all sound abruptly ceased.

Tears formed in the blood-encrusted corners of Greg's eyes. A crimson drop rolled down his cheek. It fell to the floor in seemingly slow motion, and exploded, breaking the silence.

Greg's body jerked backward.

Z realized that it was not the explosion of the tear that broke the silence, but the explosion from the barrel of the gun he held in his hand.

Z pulled the trigger once more. Greg's legs spasmed once and then his entire body went limp; lifeless.

"That's it, son," Sweet said with a smile. "Good job!"

Norm reached out a massive hand. "Now you can give me my Brad Pitt back, little nigga!"

Z thrust the pistol into his waistband and then covered it with his t-shirt. His expression was as hard and cold as the weapon pressed against his belly and the concrete under his feet.

"What the bloody hell?" Norm spat. "This little Joe Rook is bonkers!"

Sweet laid a gentle hand on Norm's arm. "Let him have it, Norm. He's earned it. I'll buy you a new one."

Sweet turned his attention to Z. "I like your style, little man. I think killing suits you and I need some killers in my camp."

Sweet pulled a large cigar from the inner pocket of his suit coat. He lit it, taking short, rapid puffs. A sweet, nutty aroma permeated the room.

"If you're willing to learn," Sweet continued, "I'm willing to make sure you learn from the best. You'll make a shitload of money, too. So, what do you say, Z?"

Sweet extended his hand. Z shook it without a word.

"Welcome to the family, Z," Sweet said. "Always remember this – nothing is lost; only, tomorrow is gained. Although you lost your *biological* father – and that hurts, I know – you didn't really lose *any*thing, Z, because *I'm* your father now!"

"*I'm your father now!*"

"*I'm your father now!*"

Ezekiel rose, bolt upright, from sleep.

"*I'm your father now,*" continued to ring in his ear. Sweat poured down his face.

"Nothing is lost; only, tomorrow is gained," Ezekiel whispered. "Or, *yesterday*. I don't know why, God, but you've given me a second chance and I am going to make things right before I go!"

CHAPTER TWELVE

Ezekiel bobbed, weaved, executed a powerful flying knee and then followed with a hooking elbow.

Sweat poured down his face, soaking his t-shirt, as he shadowboxed in the cool, noon air.

"Mr. Locke?"

Ezekiel ceased his training and looked up at the deck.

Z stood there, leaning over the railing. "Sorry to disturb you, Mr. Locke, but my parents want to know if you'd like to join us for dinner."

"What are we having?" Ezekiel asked.

"Turkey burgers and sweet potato fries," Z replied. "My favorite!"

"Mine, too!"

"Then, you'll join us?"

Ezekiel nodded. "Sure."

"Cool," Z replied. "I noticed you were shadowboxing. My dad is teaching me MMA – some boxing and Brazilian Jiu-Jitsu. What's your style?"

"Ijakadi – it's West African – but my dad taught me a little MMA too."

"Really?"

"Yeah," Ezekiel replied. "My dad was a lot like *your* dad."

"Does your father live here? In the city?" Z asked.

"He used to," Ezekiel replied. "He died when I was around your age."

"Aww, man. Sorry to hear that," Z said. "If you don't mind me asking, how did he die?"

"I don't mind," Ezekiel replied. "He was murdered."

"Murdered?" Z asked in shock. "Dang! Did the police catch who did it?"

"No. Some people my father worked for found the guy..."

Ezekiel bounded up the stairs toward Z. "They took the guy to an abandoned warehouse and...took care of everything."

"Good," Z said. "I'm glad they got some payback for your father." A mask of sadness fell over the teen's face. "Man, I don't know what I'd do if something like that ever happened to my dad."

"It won't happen to him. I promise you that. Now, let's get inside – I can smell those grilled onions from here!"

CHAPTER THIRTEEN

A dozen uniformed police officers repelled the surging crowd as Detective McGraw and his team did their work.

The detective tossed gummy bears into his mouth, savoring the chewy confections as he inspected the mangled corpses of his old associates – Frankie, Morocco, and Head.

"Somebody done killed Frankie 'nem," someone in the crowd shouted.

"Man, these polices is trippin', shawty," complained another.

Young men hoisted their girlfriends onto their shoulders to get a better view of the grisly scene over the heads of the obstructing police.

Elderly women dished the dirt from porch to porch.

Someone even sold hot chocolate, coffee, and donuts from the back of an old station wagon.

A cream-colored Rolls Royce Phantom cruised past the crowd and parked next to a row of police vehicles.

Norm stepped out of the Phantom and then opened the rear passenger's door. Danny Sweet exited the vehicle and the two men quickly approached the chain of police officers, who parted to let them through.

Detective McGraw spotted the approach of his colleagues and he greeted them with a smile. "Fellas!"

"What's the word, Terry?"

Sweet asked.

"They look like they've been in a fight with Jacky Chang on steroids," McGraw replied.

"Chan," Norm said.

"What?" McGraw asked, confused.

"Chan," Norm repeated. "It's Jacky *Chan*, not Chang."

"Chan...Chang...Ching...it all sounds like dropped silverware to me," McGraw replied, shrugging his shoulders. "Any idea who could have done this to Frankie and the boys?"

Sweet drew a cigar from the breast pocket of his suit, lit it, and raised it to his lips. The cuff of Sweet's shirt slid down his wrist. The watch he wore – a birthday present courtesy of Nigerian Norm – shined brightly in the noonday sun.

Sweet took a quick puff from the Cuban cigar and then blew the smoke over his shoulder. "The only person I know who can put in *that* kind of work with their bare hands – besides Norm – is Lala."

McGraw's eyes widened and his head snapped back. "Hold up! Lala is *real*? I thought she was just an urban legend."

"Oh, she's real," Norm replied. "Real *bonkers*! But she's not crazy enough to fuck with the Sweet Family."

"Rumor around the division is she single-handedly took out that Savannah gangster, Punch, and his whole gang without firing a shot, but I thought that was all bullshit," McGraw said.

"Yeah, that was Lala," Norm replied. "She doesn't use guns – just silent weapons, like knives, crossbows, and Eartha."

McGraw frowned and tilted his head sideways. "Eartha?"

"Eartha *Kitt*," Norm sighed. "For them what don't have a

classical education, that's '*shit*', mate."

McGraw shook his head and glanced at Sweet.

Sweet chuckled and took another drag on his cigar.

"Anyhow," Norm continued. "Lala does good work. Sweet used her once or twice."

"Yeah, but she costs an arm and a leg," Sweet said, shaking his head. "Even more than you and the rest of these badges combined, McGraw. And she's crazy as a shit-house rat! I don't like messing with her unless absolutely necessary."

Sweet pointed to the decaying bodies of his men with his cigar. "It looks like a new player's in town. Might belong to the Carver Twins."

"You thinkin' a sit down?" Norm asked.

"Definitely," Sweet answered.

"Call Caleb and have him meet us at the office. I want him to attend the sit down...you too, Terry."

Detective McGraw nodded his head. "I'm in."

"I'm going to set it up for tomorrow afternoon," Sweet said.

Norm pulled his cell-phone from its case on his belt and pressed the number two. "Hello? Hey, lemon squeezer! We got a Buster Keaton with Sweet in an hour, so heavenly the trouble and get over to the office...alright...alligator, mate."

Norm returned the phone to its case.

McGraw snapped his head from Norm, to Sweet, and then back to Norm. "Damn, I've known you for twelve years, Norm, and I still can't understand a friggin' word when you talk that Cockney shit."

"Well, if you cleaned the wax outta your sighs and had any

eighteen in your loaf," Norm began, tapping the side of his head with his fingers. "Understandin' me would be lemon squeezy, John Hop."

Detective McGraw shook his head. Sweet placed a hand on his shoulder.

"It's British Ebonics," Sweet chuckled. "You catch on after a couple decades."

Sweet pulled McGraw to him and hugged the detective. "Gotta run, Terry. See you tomorrow."

"Okay, Boss. See you tomorrow," McGraw replied. "Tomorrow, Norm."

"Alright, mate," Norm said.

Norm led Sweet through the wall of police officers. The duo hopped into the Phantom and sped off.

And watching the entire scene - from a rooftop across the street - Ezekiel made his plans.

CHAPTER FOURTEEN

"Now, *this* is good eating, baby!"

Sweet brought his face close to the plate of steaming catfish and inhaled. He closed his eyes and licked his lips as the aroma transported him back to his mama's home in Yazoo City, Mississippi; back to bare feet and fig trees and the legend of the "Chain Lady", Yazoo Witch; back to where Sweet sold his first crack rock and where he murdered his first man. "Good food, good times," he sighed.

The Sexy Woman, who sat beside Sweet, smiled. Norm nodded in agreement and devoured his food in silence.

Sweet held up a crisp, golden French fry. "Norm, tell her what you call these in England."

"Chips," Norm replied.

"Freakin' *chips*! Can you believe that?" Sweet asked. "A *chip* is a thinly sliced, flat piece of potato. Comes in different flavors, like plain – that's my favorite, barbecue, salt and vinegar – we call 'em 'salt and *sour*' back home, hot, dill pickle – I don't like them shits, though – anyway, *that's* a friggin' chip!"

Sweet snickered as he shook his head. "You English are some weird motherfuckers!"

"First of all, I'm Nigerian," Norm began.

Sweet rolled his eyes. "Here we go…"

"Second of all, no brother would ever call himself 'English', he'd say he's '*British*', and third…"

"Hold that thought," Sweet said, interrupting Norm. "I gotta take a piss."

"You're already *takin'* the piss, aren't ya'?" Norm replied.

"See…weird!" Sweet said.

The Sexy Woman smiled wider.

Sweet rose from his chair. Norm followed suit.

"Be right back, baby," Sweet said to The Sexy Woman. "Touch my fries and I'll have Norm break your fingers."

The Sexy Woman continued to smile.

Norm and Sweet left the table and walked toward the restroom.

"She doesn't say much, does she?" Norm asked.

"You see that body?" Sweet said, nodding toward the voluptuous, mocha-toned, young woman. "*That* says it *all*!"

Norm peeked over Sweet's shoulder at their table. The woman's dress was white – a prerequisite for a date with Sweet – and clung to every ample curve. Norm could only nod in agreement.

Sweet stepped into the

restroom. Norm posted himself in front of the door. The few male patrons of the restaurant who needed to relieve themselves opted to pinch their knees together and hold out a bit longer.

****

The restroom was immaculate. There wasn't even a water stain to be found on the marble floor or countertop. The fixtures were of polished brass.

"Only in Atlanta can you find a five-star, soul-food joint," Sweet snickered.

He stood in front of a urinal and unbuttoned his fly.

The door to the last stall slowly opened.

Sweet began to urinate.

Ezekiel crept out of the stall. His face was hidden by a

black ski-mask. The rest of him was covered in black as well – a black jumpsuit, black tactical boots, and black leather gloves.

He silently approached Sweet as the crime boss emptied his rather full bladder.

The feel of a cold, metal object on the back of his neck made Sweet jump. "Fuck!"

Urine splattered on the floor, just missing Sweet's white ostrich-skin shoes.

"Careful, don't piss on that nice suit," Ezekiel whispered.

"What the hell is this?" Sweet inquired. "A robbery?"

"Don't ask questions you already know the answers to," Ezekiel replied. "Now, your money and your jewelry, nigga!"

"Son, do you know who I am?"

"Yeah, a dumb motherfucker in a fancy suit. One more question and you're dead."

Sweet stuffed his genitals into his boxers and then quickly buttoned his pants. He cautiously raised his hands. "I need to reach into my suit jacket. My money is in there."

"Do it," Ezekiel hissed.

Sweet removed a gold money clip from his pocket.

Ezekiel snatched the clip from Sweet's hand. It was heavy. From the thickness of the stack of folded hundred dollar bills, Ezekiel estimated the crime boss was carrying about three thousand dollars…a good take – if it was money that he was after.

"That's all I got," Sweet whispered.

Ezekiel pushed the gun against the back of Sweet's neck and his head jerked forward forcefully.

"The jewelry, goddammit!"

Ezekiel demanded.

"I didn't wear any tonight," Sweet replied. "I plan on banging my date in the car. Rings and watches and shit get in the way."

A sharp blow to the side of the head dropped Sweet to his knees.

Ezekiel thrust his boot-heel into his victim's chest.

Sweet flew backwards and slammed into the door. He collapsed onto the floor, pressing his hand to the side of his head, as if he was trying to push down the huge edema that was growing there.

Ezekiel disappeared into the last stall.

Norm rushed into the restroom, pistol at the ready.

"Motherfucker just robbed me!" Sweet screamed as Norm pulled him up from the floor. "Last stall!"

Norm darted into the last stall. "Empty."

Norm inspected it and found a panel in the ceiling slightly out of place. "He must have escaped into the ceiling through a panel." A chill ran up Norm's spine. "Whoever he is, he's well trained. This wasn't a random robbery, Sweet."

"It's gotta be those fucking carvers," sweet spat. "nobody fucks with Danny Sweet in his city! *Nobody*!"

CHAPTER FIFTEEN

"*I remember when I met you at the ice cream parlor...you were so fine I was afraid to holler...*"

Z strummed his acoustic guitar as he sang.

"*'Cause you were coooooold...cold as a winter day.*"

Ezekiel applauded.

Lydia put down the ladle she

used to stir a big, steaming pot of chicken and rice. She clapped excitedly. "Sounds great, Z!"

"Thanks, mom," Z said. "So, what do you think, Mr. Locke?"

"Sounds really good," Ezekiel replied. "The verses are tight; the hook is nice…now, you just need to work out the bridge."

"That's just it – I can't come up with a bridge to save my life. I've tried, but I'm just not feeling it."

Z frowned and then shook his head. "Dad was supposed to help me with it, but he hasn't found the time."

"May I take a crack at it?" Ezekiel asked.

"Sure," Z answered.

Ezekiel rocked from side to side, humming different melodies. Once he decided on the melody for the bridge, he began working on the lyrics.

After ten minutes of humming and mumbling, Ezekiel nodded and smiled. "Let's try this –

You're my ice cream, baby

You're my chocolate-swirl, lady

You're my

Dulce de leche,

Café caramel latte –

You're cold…

You're cold…

You're cold…

Cold as a winter day."

Z jumped up from the couch and pumped his fist. "That's it! That's the bridge, Mr. Locke!"

Z extended his palm toward Ezekiel. Ezekiel met it with a resounding high-five.

Caleb stepped into the kitchen. The navy blue suit he wore told Lydia he was leaving to meet with Danny Sweet. She looked away from him and resumed cooking.

"Gotta run, baby," Caleb said, kissing Lydia on the cheek. "I'll be back in a little bit."

"Don't forget, Tammy is coming over to meet Jason," Lydia whispered.

"That's right! I almost *did* forget," Caleb replied under his breath. "I'll make sure I'm back in time."

Caleb walked briskly into the living room and snatched his car keys off the bookshelf. "Hey, Jason. Hey, son."

"Hey, Caleb," Ezekiel replied.

"Dad, you aren't leaving are you?" Z asked.

"Yeah, I'll be back soon, though," Caleb replied. "What's up?"

"You're supposed to help me

put together the music for Mali's art show, remember?"

"It'll have to wait until tomorrow, Z," Caleb replied. "I promise we'll get it done first thing in the morning."

Z rolled his eyes and shook his head. "That's what you said two days ago, too!"

Caleb shot Z an angry glance. The young man quickly looked away and stared at the floor.

"Watch your tone, boy!" Caleb ordered.

""Sorry, dad," Z sighed.

Caleb's face softened. He laid a hand on Z's shoulder and gently massaged it. "Son, I *promise* you...we'll get it done tomorrow, okay?"

"Alright, dad," Z replied.

"Alright, son," Caleb said. "I love you. Later."

"Love you too, dad. Later,"

Z replied.

"Be safe, Caleb," Ezekiel said.

"Always," Caleb replied, as he walked out the front door.

The door closed behind him.

Ezekiel turned back to Z, who was, once again, strumming his guitar. "Now, back to the bridge…"

CHAPTER SIXTEEN

Danny Sweet forced a smile as

he sat across the table from Virginia and Virgil Carver – the notorious Carver Twins – the only threat and obstacle to Sweet's total domination of rap and R&B music in the South and the Southeast.

Caleb, Norm, and Detective McGraw stood, menacingly, at Sweet's back.

At the Carver Twins' backs were former Navy Seals, Manny and Steve, who had been securing the Twins since Old Man Carver was still alive and running the family business and the twins were in high school.

"This is my favorite spot," Sweet proclaimed. "The food…the ambience…perfect!"

"My husband – God rest his soul – proposed to me here," Virginia Carver said. "Ah, the memories!"

"And I banged my first piece of ass here," Virgil snickered.

"In the restroom. Ah, the memories!"

Virginia punched Virgil in the arm. Virgil winced from the pain. "Ow!" he screamed, rubbing his aching bicep.

"Please, forgive my brother," Virginia said. "So, what exactly, did you want to discuss with us? It sounded urgent on the phone."

Sweet took a bite of the steaming, fried catfish that lay on the plate before him. He closed his eyes, savoring the delightful spicy-sweet flavor. "That is some good fish!"

Sweet pointed his fork in the direction of the Carver Twins and shook it as he spoke. "For ten years, we've been rivals…"

Sweet sucked a piece of fish from between his teeth and spat it into a napkin. "We first competed on these streets and now, in the music business. Congrats on signing Point Blank, by the way…he's sure to win Best New Artist at the Hip-Hop Awards. Hell, he might even give my boy, Skinz, a run for his money for Best Album."

"Thank you. We'll see," Virginia replied.

"Well, we've been bitter rivals," Sweet continued. "But we've never broken the peace with each other. There has been no violence between our families and we've all grown because of that."

Virgil glanced at his watch and then yawned.

Norm glanced at the young gangster.

Virginia shook her head.

"Look, Sweet," Virgil began. "I've got a date with a certain supermodel talk-show host in a couple of hours, so, if you don't mind…"

"Virgil!" Virginia shouted, as she placed a firm hand on her brother's forearm.

"It's okay, Virginia," Sweet said, struggling to maintain his smile. "You're right, Virgil, I'll get straight to the point."

Sweet took a deep breath. "Two nights ago, someone killed three of my best men. One of them was a Lieutenant. And then, last night, some Special Forces, ninja-type motherfucker robbed me. *Me*! Now, *that* takes balls!"

Virgil shrugged his narrow shoulders. "So, what does that have to do with us?"

Norm stepped to the table. His face twisted into a manifestation of pure rage. "We'd fuckin' like to know if you set it up, you disrespectful little wanker! That's what!"

Virgil pounded his fist on the table. Plates jumped and a few forks fell to the floor. Virgil glared at Sweet, not once acknowledging Norm's presence with his eyes. "I am Co-Boss of the Carver Family, Sweet! Since when do you allow your Captain to speak to a Boss at a sit-down?"

"Since when does a Co-Boss who rides the coattails of his sister – the *real* Boss of your family – disrespect the *Boss* of Bosses?" Sweet spat.

"The *Boss of Bosses*?" Virginia said, shaking her head. "You go too far, Sweet."

Sweet took another bite of catfish and spoke as he chewed. "Look, we both know that there isn't a Boss in the Southeast who will stand with you against me."

Sweet sprinkled hot sauce on his fish and took another bite. "But, if you *have* broken the peace, Virginia, the other Bosses *will* side with me against *you*. None of them like the idea of a female Boss, anyway. Me? I'm more progressive."

Virginia scooted her chair

away from the table and stood up. Virgil rose almost in unison with her.

Caleb and McGraw stepped forward.

Manny and Steve stood at the Carver Twins' flanks.

"This sit-down is over, Sweet!" Virginia said.

"Did you order the hit on my boys, Virginia?" Sweet asked.

"Goodbye, Sweet," Virginia said, as she walked away from the table.

The Carver Family sauntered out of the restaurant.

Sweet looked over his shoulder at his men and then waved his hands, signaling them to sit down.

"Fuckin' wankers!" Norm shouted.

"What do we do now, Sweet?" Caleb asked.

He stared out of a large window, which ran from floor to ceiling in a wall near his table. The Carver Twins were hopping into their limousine.

Sweet's upper lip curled into a sneer. "We prepare for war."

CHAPTER SEVENTEEN

The smell of garlic, onion, and bell peppers permeated the Cross house.

Ezekiel set the dining table for five as Lydia carried in a large bowl of spaghetti, a platter of garlic bread, salad, and several varieties of dressing. He wondered why the setting was for five. Were the Crosses expecting a guest? He wouldn't ask. Questions always lead to the questioner *being* questioned and the fewer questions he answered, the better.

He would catch Lydia staring at him often. He was familiar to her. Understandable, since he had come from her womb; nursed on her breasts. Thankfully, his image of himself was a bit...dark, so, upon reintegration after time travel, he did not look exactly like himself...exactly like Z. *That* would have raised eyebrows for sure.

"Thanks for lending a hand, Z!" Lydia shouted over the noise coming from the television.

Z paused his video game and craned his neck toward the dining room, "Huh?"

"I said thanks for helping out," Lydia replied.

"Oh, sorry, mom," Z said. "I'm on the last level of Changa's Safari. I'll find a save-point and come help out, though."

"It's okay," Lydia replied. "All the work is done now, anyway."

The doorbell rang.

"I've got it," Z said as he leaped from the couch.

He opened the door. A beaming smile spread across his face. "Aunt Tammy!"

A beautiful woman stood in the doorway, smiling.

"Hey, handsome," Tammy said.

Z hugged her. Tammy planted a kiss on his cheek. Z's cocoa face tinged red.

"Look at you, all grown up," Tammy said. "You got a girlfriend, or do I still have a chance?"

Z tinged even redder. He

looked away, embarrassed.

Tammy walked into the house. "Smells good in here!"

Z pushed the door to close it, but something heavy fell against it, stopping him.

Caleb peeked his head in. Z turned away from the door, rolling his eyes.

Tammy turned around and - upon seeing Caleb - her face lit up. "Hey, old man! What's up?"

Tammy and Caleb hugged.

"Same old *same* old," Caleb replied. "Been missing *you*, big head!"

"You know I had to go out of town to see Mama. She hasn't been feeling too well lately, so I decided to stay up there for a while and help out."

"Well, tell her she's in my prayers."

Tammy backed away from Caleb.

She giggled, causing her large, hoop earrings to tap a rhythm on her jaw. "Yeah, right! When was the last time you prayed, Caleb?"

"Back when they assigned you to our Recon unit," Caleb replied. "I was *praying* they'd send us somebody else!"

Tammy pushed Caleb toward the living room. "Shut up!"

They both laughed.

Lydia nudged Ezekiel into the living room.

Ezekiel quickly studied Tammy from head to toe. She was as gorgeous and sexy as he remembered. "Body like Beyonce, face like (Melanie) Fiona," he'd always say.

"Hey, Tammy," Lydia said.

"Hey, Lydia! How you doin', girl?" Tammy said, planting a kiss on her cheek.

"Good; you?"

"Pretty good."

Lydia stepped aside, opening a path between Ezekiel and Tammy. "Tammy, meet Jason Locke. Jason, meet Tammy LaRosa."

Ezekiel extended his hand. Tammy took it in hers and they shook.

"It's a pleasure to meet you, Misses…"

"*Miss*," Tammy said, cutting him off.

"*Miss* LaRosa," Ezekiel said.

"It's Tammy, Papi, and the pleasure is all mine!"

Tammy continued to hold Ezekiel's hand as she walked into the dining room. "Come on, gorgeous; we can talk while we eat. I'm starved and I *love* Lydia's cooking!"

Everyone sat at the table.

Z rubbed his palms together and licked his lips in

anticipation.

"Everyone help yourselves," Lydia said. "There's plenty."

Everyone served themselves and began devouring the delicious dinner.

Lydia nudged Caleb under the table with her elbow. Caleb looked at her with questioning eyes under raised eyebrows.

Lydia nodded toward Ezekiel.

Caleb broke the silence. "Uh, Jason…Tammy served with me in the Marines."

Ezekiel feigned surprise. "Oh, really?"

"I was the Field Medic for our Force Recon unit," Tammy replied.

"She saved my life during a mission in the Persian Gulf," Caleb said. "We've been best friends ever since."

"So, I'm sitting beside a

bonafide hero!" Ezekiel said.

"Bonafide, certified, and sanctified," Tammy said.

"So, do holy heroes drink espresso?" Ezekiel asked.

"*This* one does," Tammy replied. "Why? You got an espresso machine in your back pocket or something?"

"Nah, it's in my *other* pants," Ezekiel quipped. "Actually, I know of a nice coffeehouse, not far from here. They do live jazz there on Friday nights. Would you like to go?"

Lydia and Caleb exchanged a quick glance and smiled slyly at each other.

"I'd love to, Jason," Tammy said, blushing.

"Good," Ezekiel replied.

Ezekiel resumed eating in silence. His thoughts went to Mali. He had never dated another woman besides her. She was his first – and only – love, but somehow, this felt *right*. Maybe it was loneliness. Maybe it was all those years in Africa, training under men who had two…three…sometimes five wives – all of whom were happy. Maybe it was the fulfillment of a lifelong fantasy – dating his boyhood crush. Ezekiel wasn't sure what it was, but he was going to find out. If he ever saw his wife again, he'd make it up to her somehow.

Lydia leaned toward her husband and pressed her lips against his ear. "Operation Matchmaker is a *go*!"

CHAPTER EIGHTEEN

"Ninety-seven…ninety-eight…ninety-nine…one hundred!"

Ezekiel hopped to his feet after the last pushup. The afternoon air licked at his aching muscles and cooled the sweat on his skin.

Z walked into the backyard. He was dressed in his school's colors – black sweatpants, with a silver stripe down the side and a black hooded sweatshirt with a black and silver checkered crest on the front, in the center of which was an armored warrior-knight. 'Property of The North Atlanta School of Performing Arts' was written in silver letters below the crest. A backpack was strapped to his back. "Hey, Mr. Locke!"

"Hey, Z," Ezekiel replied. "Home from school already?"

"We had an early dismissal today, but I stayed for wrestling tryouts," Ezekiel replied.

"Congratulations," Ezekiel said.

Z frowned and squinted at Ezekiel. "Congratulations? How did you know I made the team?"

"Umm...I just figured you did. Your dad was telling me how explosive you are."

Ezekiel dropped into the splits, studying his thighs to avoid Z's gaze.

"You're pretty flexible for an old guy," Z said.

"Well, I figure if I keep myself flexible and strong and work on my cardio, maybe, just maybe I won't crumble to dust in the next couple of years."

"I guess," Z said. "Don't push yourself *too* hard, though. You might shatter a hip or something."

Ezekiel looked up at Z, prepared to hit him with a clever wisecrack, but the boy's face was blanketed with melancholy. "What's the matter, son?" he asked.

"My dad and I used to work out every day," Z sighed. "But he doesn't have time to work out – or anything else that involves me – anymore. I don't think he likes me very much."

"Don't say that!" Ezekiel said. "Caleb likes – *and* loves – you, Z. You'll realize just how much one day."

Ezekiel sat on the steps leading up to the deck. Z leaned against the banister, resting his chin on his arms.

"Your father is working hard to make ends meet and he's frustrated," Ezekiel said.

"I know," Z said. "I just want things back the way they used to be…before dad started working for Mr. Sweet."

"You're fifteen and you're bored," Ezekiel replied. "You need something to do to take your mind off of things."

Ezekiel smacked Z on the arm with the back of his hand. "You got a girlfriend?"

Z blushed. "No."

"But there *is* a girl you're interested in."

"Yeah…sorta."

"Not sorta," Ezekiel said.

"A *lot*. It's that girl you mentioned the other day…umm…Molly."

"No, it's Ma*li*," Z replied. "M-A-L-I."

"Oh, okay…Ma*li*. So, tell me about her."

"Well, her whole name is Mali Raymond," Z began. "She's my best friend; she's beautiful, pretty smile, smooth, brown skin…"

Z moved his hand in a big semi-circle, as if he was rubbing a huge globe with his palm. "…and a big old, juicy…"

"Okay, okay!" Ezekiel shouted, interrupting Z. "I get the picture! What else do you like about her besides the physical?"

"Well, she's smart," Z replied. "And she's creative, which is what I find most attractive about her."

"She's really a good artist,

huh?" Ezekiel asked.

"The best I've ever seen."

"She's all *that*?"

"All that," Z replied. "But she's good people. Not stuck up at all."

"So, why don't you ask her out? Take your friendship to the next level?"

"Two words," Z sighed. "Oliver. Hunt."

"And he is?" Ezekiel asked, hiding his clenched fists between his legs.

"Mali's boyfriend. A freshman in college. Basketball star."

"And a lame, who drinks too much and treats Mali like crap when he's drunk!" Ezekiel snapped.

"H-how…how do you know that?" Z asked, backing a step away from Ezekiel. "Mali only told *me* that stuff. No one else should know."

"I've been around a long time, Z," Ezekiel replied. "I *know* people."

"But, you never *met* Oliver...or Mali, for that matter. How could you..."

"Just drop it!" Ezekiel commanded. "I just...I just *know*, okay? Trust me!"

"Okay," Z replied. He placed a hand on Ezekiel's shoulder. "I *do* trust you, Mr. Locke."

"Then, believe me when I tell you," Ezekiel's voice became mellow once again. "You're the one Mali wants to be with. If you ask her out, she *will* say yes."

"No, she won't. She..."

Ezekiel waved his hand, dismissing Z's words. "She will say *yes*! Now, call her up. If she doesn't say yes, I'll pay you a hundred dollars."

"Okay, cool!" Z said.

"And if she does say yes, I'll drive you guys wherever you want to go," Ezekiel said. "So, you can't lose."

"Drive us?" Z asked in disbelief. "In what? Your pants pockets?"

"You're hilarious," Ezekiel said, rolling his eyes. "I'm buying a car this afternoon, smart-ass. I can't take Tammy out on the bus."

"Yeah, that would be lame," Z chuckled.

"*Very*. Now, go make that call!"

CHAPTER NINETEEN

'Coco Mocha' was full of zest and fervor – typical of a Friday night in the upscale coffeehouse.

Ezekiel and Tammy strode into Coco Mocha arm-in-arm.

Ezekiel quickly perused the establishment – the exits, the number of people, the arrangement of the tables and chairs – as he had done everywhere he visited, as he was taught to do at sixteen years of age by the jovial, but deadly, Colonel Thomas Fu-Kiau.

Ezekiel whispered praises to the Colonel and thanked God for allowing him to learn from a true military mastermind.

"This place *is* nice," Tammy said as she admired the hand-carved mahogany woodwork, the funky modern art, and the delicious aroma of hazelnut, caramel, chocolate, and Kenyan coffee.

"Told you," Ezekiel replied.

He led Tammy to a cozy two-person booth in a dimly lit corner. A vanilla-scented candle burned at the center of the table.

"Hi," a waitress said, approaching them.

"Hello," Ezekiel replied.

"Hi, sweetie," Tammy said.

"I'm Jamilah," the waitress continued. "And I'll be your server this evening. May I take your order now, or do you need a few minutes?"

"We can order now," Tammy replied. "I'll have a caramel latte with soy milk."

"Mmm...sounds good," Ezekiel said. "I'll have the same, but with two-percent milk."

"Got it!" Jamilah said. "Two caramel lattes, one with soy, one with two-percent. It'll be up in a few minutes."

Jamilah walked away from the table.

Tammy placed her palm on the back of Ezekiel's hand. Her touch was warm, soft, and feather-light. "So, Mr. Jason Locke, why is a fine, intelligent, strong brother – like you – single? Or are you?"

"I'm separated," Ezekiel replied. "I don't think I'll ever see her again, though."

"Any kids?"

"No."

"Want any?" Tammy asked,

playfully batting her eyes.

"Yes, a few," Ezekiel answered.

"A few?" Tammy echoed. "I'm good for *two*, so if we happen to get that far, you've been forewarned."

"So, what about you?" Ezekiel inquired. "Are *you* single?"

"Divorced."

"Sorry to hear that," Ezekiel lied.

"Don't be," Tammy replied. "I mean – he was a nice guy and all, but he had a bad habit. I had to let him go."

Ezekiel's eyes widened in shock. He shifted sideways in the booth, toward Tammy, in order to better study her face. "You left your husband over a bad habit? What was it? Drugs?"

"Nope," Tammy said. "Robbing banks!"

Ezekiel burst out laughing. "What?!"

"He's doing twenty-five years with no parole."

"Damn."

"Yeah," Tammy sighed, shaking her head.

Ezekiel studied Tammy closely. This woman, who watched him grow to young adulthood. This woman he knew so well, but only through the eyes of a boy -- a boy's mind - so he really barely knew her at all. And there - illuminated by the flickering of a vanilla-scented candle - he, for the first time, truly *saw* her.

"My god, you are absolutely *beautiful*!" Ezekiel said.

"Thank you," Tammy said, blushing. "It's been a long time since anyone told me that."

"I don't believe that."

"I mean - guys tell me I'm

sexy as hell…I'm gorgeous…I got a bangin'-ass body…and they're right…"

Ezekiel laughed. "Aw come on, Tammy. Don't be so modest!"

"Whatever," Tammy said, smiling. "But, seriously…'beautiful'? Not too many brothers tell me that. In fact, you're the *only* one."

"Well, I speak truth," Ezekiel replied. "You're…Blacknificent!"

Tammy laughed. "Blacknificent, huh? Clever; I like that!"

"Thank you," Ezekiel replied, as he patted himself on the back with his fingers.

"You can truly know a man's mind by the words he chooses to use," Tammy said, leaning closer to Ezekiel.

They sat in silence for a moment, studying each other's

faces.

"Jason," Tammy whispered. "After we have our drinks, I would very much like for you to accompany me home."

"You don't want dessert?" Ezekiel asked.

"*That's* why I want you to come home with me," Tammy replied. "So you can have your cake…"

"And eat it, too?" Ezekiel said, smiling slyly.

"I insist," Tammy said.

Ezekiel turned from Tammy and waved his hands high above his head until he caught Jamilah's attention.

"Yes, sir?" Jamilah asked as she approached their booth. "How may I help you?"

Ezekiel handed Jamilah a twenty-dollar bill. "Can you make those lattes to go, please? Quickly? Please?"

Tammy rested her head upon Ezekiel's shoulder and laughed – huskily, seductively – into his ear.

CHAPTER TWENTY

Ezekiel awakened wrapped in cinnamon-scented sheets.

Tammy's king-sized bed was comfortable enough to stay in all day, whether reading a good book or making great love.

Ezekiel sat up and sniffed the air. The smell of buttered bread, fresh fruit, and hot maple syrup beckoned him out of bed.

He stepped out of Tammy's bedroom and then strolled down the long hallway to the winding staircase at the end of it. Tammy's bank-robbing husband – it appeared – had taken good care of her. Ezekiel realized that although his father and Tammy were best friends, he had never been to her house. Perhaps his father had, but he had never mentioned it. There was much to learn about Tammy, and Ezekiel intended to explore every bit of her.

As he entered the kitchen, Tammy met him with a warm hug and a soft kiss.

"Good morning, sleepy-head," Tammy said.

"Morning," Ezekiel replied.

Tammy took Ezekiel's hand and led him to her breakfast nook. The cozy, little area faced a Japanese-style pond, which was filled with large koi. The colorful fish flitted around the surface of the pond, creating a beautiful, liquid rainbow.

On the table were two plates – one had raisin toast, two slices of fresh mango, and a bowl of oatmeal – "Obviously Tammy's," Ezekiel thought. The other was loaded with a stack of pancakes, a bowl of grits, and four turkey sausage patties.

"Damn," Ezekiel said, licking his lips. "You always cook like this?"

"Only for a man who makes love as incredibly as you did last night," Tammy replied.

Ezekiel blushed.

"You *would* have gotten breakfast in bed," Tammy continued. "If you had been *amazing* and not just incredible."

"I promise to do better next time."

"Oh, yeah?" Tammy asked, as she wrapped her arms around Ezekiel's thick neck. "And when is 'next time' gonna be?"

"I'm thinking right after breakfast," Ezekiel replied.

"I'm thinking *during* breakfast," Tammy said.

"Even better."

Ezekiel pulled Tammy to him and kissed her passionately. She

returned the kiss with even more
fire and Ezekiel knew that this
would be the best breakfast he
ever had in his life.

CHAPTER TWENTY-ONE

The afternoon sun shone through Danny Sweet's office window, illuminating the stark whiteness within.

Sweet sat, almost invisible, in his chair, matching his alabaster surroundings like a chameleon.

In contrast, Norm sat on the other side of Sweet's desk, dressed in an indigo linen suit.

Sweet picked up his cell-phone and typed in a phone number.

"*Hello?*" It was Lydia's voice on the phone.

"Hey, beautiful," Sweet replied.

"*Oh, hey, Sweet,*" Lydia said dryly. "*I'll get Caleb for you.*"

"Hold on, Lydia. No need to rush. How have you been?"

"*Busy.*"

"Still teaching those retards at Crown Elementary, huh?"

"*I'm still teaching* special education*, yes.*"

"You can come work for me, Lydia. I'll pay you better than the public school system ever would."

"*I'm sure. I* could *come teach Norm. He seems to be in need of special education.*"

Norm frowned and leaned forward in his chair. "What?

What the bloody hell did she say?"

"Hi, Norman," Lydia chirped.

Norm sat back in his chair and inhaled deeply, controlling the anchor rising in his chest.

"Okay, Lydia, I see you got jokes, as always," Sweet said. "It was good talking to you, beautiful. May I speak to Caleb now?"

"Just a moment," Lydia replied. *"Caleb? Caleb, honey…telephone!"*

"Hello?"

"Caleb! What's up?" Sweet inquired.

"What's up, Sweet? How you doin'?"

"I'm just coasting the fast lane, baby!" Sweet replied. "I need you to come down to the office ASAP. I got a job for you."

"A job? Don't I already work

for you?"

"Everybody got jokes today," Sweet snickered. "I'm talking about a *special* assignment. I need somebody I can trust on this one."

"Alright, Sweet. I'm on my way."

"Okay, Caleb. See you soon."

Sweet slipped the phone into his blazer pocket and turned his attention to Norm. "Call Tony Grillo and tell him we're ready to deal."

"Set it up for tonight?" Norm asked.

"Yeah. The Hip-Hop Awards are tomorrow night," Sweet replied. "I need the shit like yesterday."

"I'm on it!"

Norm picked up the office phone and began to dial.

CHAPTER TWENTY-TWO

Caleb walked into Sweet's office. Norm greeted him with a nod. Sweet greeted him with a warm smile.

"Come on in and sit down, Caleb," Sweet said.

Caleb shook Sweet's hand and sat across the desk from him.

"How are you, Caleb?" Sweet asked.

"Great," Caleb replied. "What's up?"

"As you know, tomorrow is the Hip Hop Awards," Sweet began. "Everybody and their mama is gonna be there. With the recent misunderstanding between us and the Carver Family, some nasty shit might go down and we wanna be ready."

"Ready?" Caleb said. "You have me, McGraw, and Nigerian Norm watching your back. It don't get no better than *that*, Sweet!"

"Right!" Norm agreed.

"I know y'all are the hardest hitting motherfuckers *in* this city," Sweet replied. "But the Carver Twins seem to have a dangerous player on their team. We need a little more firepower."

"What do you need me to do, then?" Caleb asked.

"We got a connection; his name is Tony Grillo," Sweet said. "He sells guns. Got a nice deal for us too."

Sweet turned his attention to Norm, who sat a couple yards from Caleb. Norm held a loaded backpack in his lap.

"Give him the money, Norm," Sweet said.

"Think fast!" Norm said, tossing the bag toward Caleb's face.

Caleb snatched the bag out of the air.

"There's twelve grand in that bag," Sweet began. "The location of the meet is in there too."

"Cool," Caleb said, nodding his head.

"Tony should be giving you three AR-Fifteens, two MP-Fives and two silencers for the MP-Fives," Sweet continued. "I want you to meet me back here tomorrow afternoon with the merchandise. Around two o'clock should be good."

"Got it," Caleb said, rising from his chair. "See you tomorrow."

"Two o'clock," Sweet reiterated.

Caleb nodded and left the office.

"Maybe, after this, I'll get that raise," he whispered, as he entered the elevator.

A smile spread across Caleb's face as he stepped out of the lobby of the Sweet South Records building and into the cool, night air.

CHAPTER TWENTY-THREE

Ezekiel moved around in a wide circle, shifting his weight from his left to his right as he held the Thai striking pads.

Z mirrored Ezekiel's movement as he punished the pads with sharp punches and kicks.

Ezekiel noticed movement in his peripheral vision. He snapped his head toward the movement.

Caleb and Tammy had entered the backyard and were quietly observing Ezekiel and Z's training session.

Ezekiel nodded, acknowledging the presence of his lover and his father.

Caleb returned the acknowledgment with a nod of his own. Tammy wiggled her fingers, playfully waving at her man.

"Put more hip into it boy, like I showed you!" Caleb shouted.

Z glanced toward his father and then returned to working the pads. "Dad, if I hit too hard, I might hurt Mr. Locke."

Ezekiel lowered his hands and backed away from Z, bringing pause to their workout. "Hurt me? Showing off in front of Tammy and your daddy, huh?"

"Well, you never want to spar," Z said. "I figure it's because you're a little intimidated by contact...*especially* from somebody on *my* level."

"And what level is that?" Ezekiel asked.

Z raised an eyebrow and smirked. "You really wanna know?"

"Yep," Ezekiel replied.

Z raised his fists and tucked his chin, assuming a boxer-like fighting stance. "I can *show* you better than I can tell you."

Ezekiel tossed the pads into the grass. "Then, *please*, *show* me!" He assumed a deep fighting position of his own.

"Don't hurt him *too* badly, Z," Tammy shouted. "We're having lunch later!"

Ezekiel and Z squared off.

Z exploded forward with a flurry of punches.

Ezekiel deftly parried and evaded the strikes and then countered with a jumping knee to Z's chin.

Z side-stepped, just barely avoiding the powerful knee strike. Wind, generated by the force of the blow, whipped across Z's face.

The young man feigned an

uppercut punch.

Ezekiel jerked his head backward to dodge the blow.

Z quickly followed the fake with a straight punch that crashed into Ezekiel's jaw.

Ezekiel rolled with the punch, turning his head in the direction of the force in order to soften the blow.

Z leaped forward and wrapped his arm around the back of Ezekiel's head. He then grabbed his wrist, pulling the radius bone up into Ezekiel's throat.

Z smiled and winked at his father as he squeezed the guillotine-choke tighter around Ezekiel's neck.

His smile quickly faded, however, as Ezekiel pressed his palms against Z's knees, locking the boy's legs straight.

Ezekiel rolled backward, keeping his arms extended. Z flew

over Ezekiel's head.

The boy's back slammed onto a mound of dirt.

Ezekiel continued rolling until his knees were straddled across Z's waist.

Ezekiel followed up with a bone-wrenching shoulder-lock, bending Z's arm at an odd angle.

Z winced in pain. He slapped the ground three times with his palm, indicating surrender.

Ezekiel released Z and then helped the boy to his feet.

Caleb and Tammy looked at each other. Tammy raised an eyebrow. Caleb shrugged.

"Didn't see *that* one coming did you?" Ezekiel chuckled.

"Yo, Mr. Locke, you *got* to teach me that!" Z said, excitedly.

"I got you, little brother," Ezekiel replied. "We'll work on it tomorrow morning."

"Cool!" Z said.

Ezekiel picked up the pads and sauntered toward Tammy.

Z ran to his father.

Caleb held his palms above his head. Z slapped his father's palms with his own.

"Damn, son," Caleb said, smiling proudly. "You've gotten great!"

"I've been working hard on what you taught me, Dad," Z replied. "Looking forward to my next lesson."

"As soon as I get some time, Z, I promise," Caleb sighed.

Z's elated expression faded for a moment, but quickly returned. "Dad, I got a new track that I'm gonna spit lyrics to. You wanna hear it?"

"Yeah, I got a minute," Caleb replied. "Let's go!"

Caleb and Z sprinted to the front of the house and went inside.

****

"So, Jason…" Tammy began. "Why – and where – does a funeral arranger learn to fight like that?"

"Arranging funerals is a dangerous business," Ezekiel replied. "So, I picked up a few things here and there over the years."

"Mmm-hmm," Tammy hummed, pursing her lips.

Ezekiel grabbed Tammy and kissed her, praying that such a spontaneous and sensual move would distract her from further questioning about his martial prowess.

"So, where are we going for

lunch?" he asked.

"What do you have a taste for?" Tammy asked.

"You," Ezekiel replied.

"You can have me anytime," Tammy said. "Besides *me*, what do you have a taste for?"

"Well, I haven't had Thai food in a while," Ezekiel said.

"I know just the place."

"Let's go!"

Ezekiel headed toward the front of the house. Tammy grabbed his arm, stopping Ezekiel in his tracks.

"We go *after* you hit the showers, buddy," she said. "You're kind of tart."

Ezekiel pulled Tammy to him and grabbed her in a headlock, pulling her face into his armpit. "You know you love this manly scent!"

Tammy pushed Ezekiel's arm and tried to wiggle her head free from his grasp. "Oh, God, you're killing me!"

Tammy suddenly wrapped her arms around Ezekiel's waist. She thrust her hips forward, against his thigh, which off-balanced him. Tammy then arched her back and twisted to the side, slamming Ezekiel to the ground.

Ezekiel's eyes widened in shock. He stared at Tammy in amazement.

"I picked up a few things here and there, too," she said, pressing her body on top of Ezekiel's.

"What else do you know how to do?" Ezekiel asked, as he slid his palms down her back.

"Let me show you."

Tammy nibbled Ezekiel's lip, signaling him to present his tongue. She then slid her full lips down the length of his tongue

until their lips touched and they
kissed as if they were trying to
consume one another.

CHAPTER TWENTY-FOUR

Z stood next to his father, inspecting his attire in the mirror while Caleb shaved.

"Where are you going, dad?" Z asked.

"I have to take care of some business for Mr. Sweet," Caleb replied.

Z adjusted his fitted cap, ensuring it was tilted at just the right angle. "Will you be home by the time I get back from my date with Mali? I want to fill you in on all the juicy details!"

"I'm not sure," Caleb replied. "If I'm not back, just tell your mother. She'll fill me in."

Z's chin sank toward his chest and his lips curled downward in a frown. "Okay," he sighed.

Caleb scooted past his son and then headed toward the front door.

Ezekiel stepped into the hallway, blocking Caleb's path.

"Whoa, Jason, you startled me!" Caleb said.

"Your son really looks up to you," Ezekiel replied. "He would give the world just to spend a day with you."

"I wish I had that kind of time," Caleb said. "Sweet keeps me busy and…"

"Too busy for your son?" Ezekiel said, interrupting Caleb. "You don't want to lose Z to these streets. He's a good…"

"I *know* what my son is, Jason!" Caleb shouted. "How and when I spend time with my kid is my business!"

Caleb's visage was one of barely controlled rage. "I like you, Jason, but please, watch your mouth when it comes to how I raise my son!"

Ezekiel and Caleb stared each

other down.

After a tense moment, Ezekiel nodded and stepped aside. "Whatever you say, Caleb. Enjoy your meeting."

Caleb stormed out of the house, slamming the door behind him.

Ezekiel turned to walk back to the kitchen. Z stood before him.

"Thanks, for trying," Z said.

"Any time."

"I wish my dad would take an interest in music again," Z sighed. "He's really talented."

"I know he is," Ezekiel replied. "I think he stays away from all that because he knows how dirty the music industry has become."

"That's why it has to be cleaned up – from the inside – by the artists!" Z said. "When I blow up, I'm gonna change the music – make it *mean* something again."

"You're gonna blow up when you grow up, huh?" Ezekiel said.

"Oh, I'm ill right *now*," Z boasted. "I have a few songs already done and they're *hot*! I'm gonna ask dad to give my demo to Mr. Sweet and then…"

"Stay away from Sweet, Z!" Ezekiel ordered.

He placed a hand on his younger self's shoulder. "Sweet will take your talent and turn it…turn *you* into something…else."

"Okay, Mr. Locke. If you say so," Z replied. "Shoot, there are gonna be plenty companies beating down my door in a minute anyway."

"You're good, but are you really *that* good?"

"The best."

"Okay, I want to hear that

demo, then," Ezekiel said. "We'd better get going, though. You don't want to keep Mali waiting – and we have to scoop Tammy on the way."

"Alright, I'm ready," Z replied. "Man, I cannot believe Mali actually said yes!"

"I told you!"

"Yeah, and I am so glad you proved me wrong!"

CHAPTER TWENTY-FIVE

The crowd poured out of the theater. The shocking ending of '*Patient is the Hunter*' was the topic of everyone's conversation. Z and Mali were no exception.

"Man, the ending really *got* me," Mali said. Her voice was a husky alto and mature beyond her years. "I was not expecting *that*!"

Z laughed and squeezed Mali's hand gently. "You were terrified! I've never seen anybody so scared in my life!"

"Me? You looked like you were about to cry," Mali chuckled. "You and Ms. LaRosa."

Z looked around, craning his neck in an effort to see over the thick crowd to the parking lot. "Where are they, anyway? They should have pulled up by now."

"I don't know," Mali replied, shrugging her shoulders. "They're probably doin' it."

"Well, if they are, I hope they're not in the back seat, since *we* have to sit back there," Z said.

"Eww," Mali cried, scowling in disgust.

Z gazed at Mali, amazed at the depth of her beauty. She was the total opposite of the other pretty, permed-out, high-maintenance girls he knew. Mali was earthy. She wore no makeup or jewelry, except large, silver hoop earrings; she sported a wild afro, which Z often referred to as a black ball of fire atop her head; and she shunned short skirts and high heels for ankle length denim skirts and combat boots. While other girls were working on cheers or discussing the latest fashions with their friends, Mali was working on a painting, or practicing with her acoustic guitar.

"Well, since we're waiting…" Z crooned.

Mali looked at him with amused curiosity. "What?"

Z pulled Mali's chest to his and stared into her eyes.

"If we do this," Mali whispered. "Things between us will change."

"How so?" Z asked.

"You'll be my *boy*friend, not just my best friend."

"Good."

Mali closed her eyes. Z slowly brought his lips closer to Mali's.

****

From Ezekiel's car, he and Tammy observed the young couple.

"Check Z out," Tammy chuckled.

"*Too* smooth!" Ezekiel replied.

****

Z's heart jumped as his lips touched Mali's full, moist ones.

"*Mali!*"

Mali and Z jerked apart from each other at the sound of the incensed voice.

The couple snapped their heads in the direction of the voice.

"Oliver," Mali gasped.

Oliver Hunt stood before them. Two of Oliver's friends – obviously athletes, by their sinewy builds and assured demeanor – stood at his flank.

Oliver exploded forward and drove his palms into Z's chest.

Z stumbled backward a few yards.

"Ollie, don't!" Mali screamed.

"Mali, what the hell is going on?" Oliver asked, sneering at his girlfriend. "You're cheating on me with *this* lame?"

"This is Z; my…best friend," Mali replied.

"The little faggy kid?" Ollie shouted. "Have you lost your damned mind?"

Oliver grabbed Mali's wrist and yanked her toward him. "Come on…let's go!"

Ezekiel pulled up close to the scene of the conflict. The theatergoers had gathered around, hoping for some real-life violence to complement the on-screen violence they had just witnessed.

Z spotted Ezekiel's car. He questioned Ezekiel with his eyes, asking if it would be okay to fight back. Ezekiel nodded, his eyes saying, "Beat. Them. Down."

"Let her go, Oliver!" Z ordered. "You don't have to do her like that!"

Oliver released Mali and then he and his friends began circling Z, like a pack of jackals circling a wounded rabbit.

"Run along, little boy, before you get hurt!" Oliver said.

"I don't think so," Z replied.

Oliver's tallest friend – at least a half-foot taller than Z – stomped and then angrily spat on the cool concrete. "Man, Ollie, let's smash this nigga!"

"Hell yeah," Oliver's other friend agreed.

"See, you had the chance to leave in peace," Oliver said. "Now you leave…"

"In pieces," Z said, interrupting Oliver. "For real, dude? Are you serious? In *pieces*? That's a hell of a cliché, dude."

"What?!" Oliver screamed. "Let's *kill* this sarcastic-ass nigga!"

"Oliver, please…stop!" Mali pleaded.

"Shut up, ho'!" Oliver replied. "I'll deal with you later!"

"*Later*, you'll be at the hospital getting my Jordan's

surgically removed from your ass," Z said.

Oliver growled as he charged toward Z.

Z sidestepped – avoiding Oliver's bull-like rush – and then whipped a pulverizing round-kick into Oliver's thigh.

Oliver collapsed onto his face.

The shorter of Oliver's friends grabbed Z around the waist, hoisted him high into the air and slammed him to the ground.

Z winced as flesh collided with concrete.

Fighting the piercing pain in his lower back and shoulder blades, Z thrust his feet forward while exploding from the ground with his hips.

The short jock screamed as his kneecaps shattered. The man fell to the ground, driven to unconsciousness by unbearable pain.

Z rolled backward and then popped up onto his feet.

Oliver rose from the ground and charged Z from the side as his tall friend hurtled toward Z's chest.

Z bent his knees deeply and then exploded upward and forward with an elbow strike to the tall man's chin.

A moist, crunching noise issued from the tall man's face. The jock collapsed where he stood and lay - unmoving - on the cold concrete.

Oliver threw a wild, looping punch with all the strength he could muster, hoping to get lucky and connect with a part of Z's face that would knock the boy silly, if not unconscious.

Luck, however, was not on Oliver Hunt's side. Z slipped under the punch, allowing it to whip over his head. He then grabbed Oliver's arm and pivoted behind him, forcing the jock's wrist between his own legs.

Z yanked up on Oliver's wrist, slamming the bully's forearm into his testicles.

Oliver's legs turned to noodles as his testicles were driven up into his belly. He fell to the ground, rolling from side to side and moaning weakly.

Mali ran to Z and hugged him. Z leaned forward and kissed her tenderly on the lips.

"Hey, boyfriend," Mali whispered.

"I like the sound of that," Z replied.

"Screw both of y'all!" Oliver shouted as he struggled to his feet. "Enjoy that nigga while you can, bitch!"

Oliver threw up both middle fingers and then sprinted toward the street.

A moment later, there was the screeching of tires...the sickening thud of metal meeting flesh...and screams of terror and disgust.

"Oh, my God!" Mali gasped as she witnessed Oliver's limp and tattered body tumble and slide down the street, leaving bits of flesh and bone behind him.

Z's mouth dropped and a tear fell from the corner of his eye. "No!"

Ezekiel and Tammy sprang from the car.

Tammy ran to render assistance to Oliver as Ezekiel sprinted toward Mali and Z.

"Mr. Locke, he...I..." Z stuttered.

"It's not your fault, son," Ezekiel said as he embraced his younger self and his future wife. "It's not *either* of your faults."

Tammy looked up from Oliver's twisted body and locked eyes with

Ezekiel. She shook her head, indicating that Oliver was now beyond help.

Ezekiel nodded and then closed his eyes. He took a deep breath and then listened to the thoughts swirling in his head. "Mali not blind. No paradox? I *can* change things. No paradox! No *alternate* reality – just...*reality*. I. Can. Change. Things! I...can...*change*..."

CHAPTER TWENTY-SIX

Caleb slapped a magazine into his pistol and then racked the slide, putting a bullet into the chamber. He pressed his chest to the steering wheel and slipped the gun into a holster at the base of his spine.

Out the windshield, he studied the area. A short, husky man, with olive skin and short, curly, auburn hair, leaned against a black SUV. No one else was in sight, but on a deal like this, Caleb knew that others were somewhere near - waiting in shadow - in case things went badly. He, on the other hand, was alone. He preferred it that way. Years as a Marine sniper had accustomed Caleb to relying on just himself to carry out a mission.

He exited his vehicle, throwing the backpack full of cash across his shoulder.

Caleb approached the olive-skinned man slowly, listening for any movement, any sign of the others. Nothing. They were well-trained. "Tony Grillo?"

"That's me," the man replied. "You must be Sweet's guy."

"Yeah, my name's Caleb."

"What you got for me, Caleb?"

Caleb handed the backpack to Grillo, who unzipped the bag and peered into it, perusing its contents. He nodded his approval and placed the heavy backpack on the ground.

"So, Caleb, what's Sweet doin'?" Grillo asked. "Sendin' some rappers to Afghanistan to fight a freakin' war or something?"

"Don't know," Caleb replied. "Are the weapons in your vehicle? I'll load them up while you count the money."

"How are you gonna load them with cuffs on?" Grillo inquired.

A chill clawed its way up Caleb's spine. "What?!"

Grillo drew his pistol and aimed it at Caleb's forehead. "A-T-F! Hands up! Hands...*up*!"

A squad of ATF agents burst from the shadows, pointing pistols and assault rifles in Caleb's direction.

Caleb slowly raised his hands and interlaced his fingers on top of his head. "Shit!"

CHAPTER TWENTY-SEVEN

The interrogation room was sweltering. Streams of sweat rolled down Caleb's forehead and seared his eyes. Caleb instinctively attempted to bring his hands to his eyes to rub away the pain, but his wrists were cuffed to the arms of his chair.

Grillo entered the room. He pulled a paper towel from his back pocket and wiped the sweat from Caleb's eyes. "Is that better?"

Caleb answered the question with silence and a hard glare.

"Have you considered our offer, Mr. Cross?" Grillo asked.

"I ain't no snitch, Agent

Grillo."

"That's *Special* Agent," Grillo replied with a smile. "With the attempted purchase of an illegal arsenal, plus the unregistered weapon you were carrying, you're looking at fifteen years, easy."

"Fifteen years, my ass," Caleb replied. "I'm a decorated veteran of the Gulf War. Silver Star recipient. Honorable Discharge. Sweet's lawyers will murder you in court!"

"So, you'd never snitch on one of yo' *home*boys, huh?" Grillo said, affecting a rapper's speech as he posed in a mocking 'B-Boy' stance.

Caleb sneered at the ATF special agent with disgust. "Are you serious with that racist bullshit?"

"I mean…never ever, ever, ever, ever, ever, ever, never?" Grillo asked with a chuckle.

"Add another 'ever' if you want, goddammit! The answer is still *hell* no!"

"Not even on a man who wants to make you look like crap in front of your wife so she loses respect for *you* and turns her sights toward *him*?"

"What the hell are you talking about?"

Grillo slid a small, thin digital voice recorder from the pocket of his windbreaker and placed it on the desk in front of Caleb. "This is from a call we intercepted from Sweet's cell-phone a few months ago."

Grillo pressed play on the recorder and Sweet's voice slithered out of the speaker.

"*Yeah, he's good, Norm, but I'm not paying him a penny more!*"

"*I'm just saying, Caleb does good work -- he brings a lot to the table.*"

"And he agreed to work for the low-low, so…"

"I can't believe the wanker was dumb enough to take what you offered him."

"Not dumb…desperate. After Caleb got out of the Marines, he couldn't find a job."

"Yeah, blokes ain't exactly lookin' to put an assassin on the payroll."

"Exactly. The nigga came crawling to me, begging for a job. I hired him so Lydia would know that I am the provider in her house. Whether they eat depends on me. I want them both to know that I'm the better man and that bitch should have married me!"

"Damn, Boss, that's some diabolical shit! I like it!"

Norm and Sweet laughed heartily.

Special Agent Grillo stopped the recording and sat back in his chair.

Caleb stared at the digital tape recorder as if he expected it to come to life and tell him this was all some cruel practical joke.

After a long silence, Caleb looked up and locked eyes with Grillo. "Okay, what do you need me to do?"

CHAPTER TWENTY-EIGHT

The phone rang.

"Sweet South Records. This is Danny Sweet."

"*Hey, Sweet. It's Caleb.*"

"Caleb! My brother! Where you at?"

"*I just pulled into the garage. I'll be up in a sec'.*"

"You got the shit?"

"*Yeah.*"

"Good. Put it in the Phantom

and pull up front. I rented a couple of suites at the W for our Hip-Hop Awards after-party. I wanna check the layout."

"Alright."

"We'll be right down, Caleb. Peace."

"Peace."

Sweet hung up the phone and turned to Norm, who was busy polishing his Stacy Adams with a handkerchief.

"Let's go, Norm," Sweet said. "I got a feeling that tonight, we're gonna make history!"

CHAPTER TWENTY-NINE

The smell of ink and the shrill buzz of a tattoo machine welcomed Ezekiel as he strode into 'cARTel Tattoos'.

A young woman reclined in an oversized black leather chair. Her shirt was open, revealing beautiful, dark-chocolate breasts.

A man leaned over the woman, turning her left breast into a scoop of fudge ice cream, with a cherry on top, with skillful manipulations of the tattoo machine.

The man looked up. Ezekiel recognized him. Greg Blake, his first kill. The man who murdered Ezekiel's father.

Greg Blake smiled. Ezekiel beat back the urge to leap forward and kick out his teeth.

"How you doin', bruh?" Greg asked with an upward tilt of his chin.

"Fine, you?"

"Fantastic!" Greg said, returning to his transformation of the woman's breast. "You here for a tat'?"

"Yes," Ezekiel replied.

"Okay, have a seat and I'll hook you up in a minute," Greg replied. "We're almost done here."

Ezekiel sat down on a red leather couch and threw his feet up on the matching ottoman. "Thanks."

Once again, thoughts swirled about Ezekiel's head like fireflies. "Just fifteen years old. First kill. Eye for an eye. Greg Blake. Father. I'm your father. Sweet. Norm. Pain. Kill…"

Ezekiel's thoughts carried him back to his second kill. He had just completed his training under Norm and had to have a kill under his belt before Master Chagga Mutwa would accept him as a disciple.

Knowing that it was the Carver Twins who hired Greg Blake to kill his father, Ezekiel decided he would make an impression on Master Mutwa by bringing him two heads, not one.

Manny, Steve, and the Carver

Twins were at V & V Recording – the studio owned by the Carvers. They were bobbing their heads to the kinetic rhythm of the rapper Point Blank's new song, 'Fuck the Feds'.

Point Blank stood in the recording booth, delivering his lyrics through a gilded sneer.

"Time to get drastic

Fuck the bastard

Here's the tape,

Wrap that nigga up in plastic

And we'll stick him with the last kid,

Under them tires

Hold up,

This nigga's wired

Set him on fire!

Now, he's lookin' like the Ghost Rider

Here's my Cuban

I'm a' use this nigga like a lighter

Get the fluid

And ignite the flames a little higher

Bring the burgers

Make a barbecue outta murder...

F-B-I?

Fuck them niggas!

C-I-A?

Fuck them niggas!

N-S-A?

Fuck them niggas!

D-E-A?

Fuck them..."

Z burst into the studio. He fired two quick shots.

One bullet struck Manny between his eyebrows.

Blood and brain splashed into

Steve's face, blinding him to the round that struck *him* in the throat, nearly severing his head upon exit.

Manny and Steve fell; their service to the Carver family terminated by blood and bone.

Point Blank dropped to the floor of the recording booth and pressed his back against the door to block the shooter's entry into the booth.

Virginia exploded forward and slapped Z's gun as she struck a nerve plexus in his wrist. The pistol flew out of his hand and slid under the studio's mixing board.

Virgil whipped a roundhouse kick into Z's abdomen. The powerful blow sent him flying backward.

Z slammed into the wall behind him. Flecks of drywall fell - like snowflakes - upon his shoulders.

The Carvers rushed toward him in a synchronized, zigzagging shuffle.

Z leaped forward and then threw a straight punch at Virgil while simultaneously thrusting a back kick at Virginia.

The kick landed home, hammering into Virginia's collarbone.

Virginia staggered backward, one arm flailing, lifeless, against her thigh.

The punch missed, however, and whizzed harmlessly past Virgil's nose.

Virgil quickly countered with a palm strike to Z's solar plexus.

Air whooshed from the young assassin's mouth and he collapsed onto one knee.

Virginia slammed a knee into Z's back. He swallowed a scream as he felt his shoulder blade split in two.

Z's vision blurred. His mind tried desperately to collapse in upon itself in order to escape the agonizing pain, which crept across his back and up his neck.

Desperate, the boy rolled toward the mixing board. He collapsed onto his belly and – with shaking fingers – reached for his pistol.

Virgil leaped in the air, poised to drive his knee down into the boy's spine and cut his career as an assassin short.

Z grabbed the gun, rolled onto his belly and fired.

The bullet tore through the bottom of Virgil's chin. A split second, the back of the crime Boss' head burst open, painting the ceiling red and gray.

Z fired again.

The round struck Virginia in the chest.

She collapsed. Her lifeless

body fell, with a thud, upon the corpse of her twin.

Z stumbled out of the studio and fell against a wall in the hallway.

The janitor – a burly, old man, who reeked of stale wine – dropped his buffer and ran to Z. "Hey! Hey, man! You okay?"

"Hey! Hey, man! You okay?"

The voice was different. Younger...less gruff...not the janitor...Greg Blake.

Ezekiel squeezed his eyelids together tightly and then opened his eyes wide to regain his focus. Greg Blake stood over him. The woman with the fudge sundae breast was gone.

"You okay, brother?" Greg asked.

"Yeah, I'm fine," Ezekiel replied. "Just lost in thought."

"So, what kind of tat' do you

want?" Greg handed Ezekiel a photo album full of tribal designs and illustrations. "We have a special on custom tats that I know you'll…"

Ezekiel laid the photo album next to him on the couch. "Actually, I came here to *talk*."

"Talk? To *me*? About?"

"About turning down that assignment the Carver Twins gave you," Ezekiel answered.

Greg Blake frowned. His forehead wrinkled and his eyes shrank to slivers. "Huh? I don't know what you're talking about."

"Oh, no?" Ezekiel said, leaning forward and flashing a wry smile. "Your name is Gregory Aldous Blake; you're a hell of a tattoo artist, but you're something…else, aren't you? You're an ex-CIA wet-boy, an assassin. This business is just a cover for your freelance wet-work. Know what I'm talking about now?"

Greg sat back down on his stool. "Naw, man, I don't."

Ezekiel snatched the photo album from the couch and hurled the heavy book at Greg's head.

Instinctively, Greg evaded the photo album and caught it with one hand. Not once did he take his eyes off of Ezekiel, who raised an eyebrow and smiled knowingly.

"Okay, let's say I *am* all that you say," Greg said. "Then I'd probably kill you unless you told me how the hell you know about me."

"I'll tell you this," Ezekiel replied. "The Carvers paid you to kill Caleb Cross for working with 'Sweet' Danny Sweet. Sound about right?"

"Fuck no!" Greg replied. "If I *am* the man you think I am, and if I *was* paid to kill Caleb Cross, it wouldn't have been the Carver Twins who paid me, it would have been Sweet."

"Bullshit!"

"Naw, nigga," Greg snickered. "That's *real* shit!"

"Why would Sweet do that?"

"Because this Caleb Cross guy is a snitch. Sweet was arrested yesterday. Don't you watch the news, fool?"

"I try not to," Ezekiel replied.

Greg laughed mockingly. A mist of spittle sprayed from his mouth. "Kind of screws up *your* plans doesn't it. Got a Plan B, chump?"

"That's not important," Ezekiel answered. "What *is* important is you don't go through with the hit on Caleb Cross."

"And if I do?"

Ezekiel smiled slyly and sat back with his fingers interlaced behind his head. "Well, I'll tell you what else I know. I know that your wife, Claudette, and your daughter, Diane, live with you at 8624 Marbut Road, in Stone Mountain. I know that they are watching cartoons in your bedroom, like they do every day at this time. 'Bino and Fino' is little Diane's favorite, right?"

"You son-of-a-bitch!" Greg screamed as he leaped to his feet.

"I also know that you keep your pistol in the middle drawer at your workstation," Ezekiel said calmly as he pulled his own pistol from its holster. He pointed the gun at Greg's chest. "My gun, however, is right here."

Greg forced his angry expression to soften and then he sat back down.

"I can kill *you*," Ezekiel continued. "And then I can take a quick drive to 8624 Marbut Road, *or* I can just disappear. The choice is yours."

"What is this Caleb Cross to you?" Greg asked. "Why are you taking such a big risk for that snitch? Is he your boyfriend or something?"

"That 'snitch' is my father."

"Bullshit! He looks *your* age!"

"I matured early," Ezekiel said.

He rose and walked, backward, toward the exit, keeping his eyes on Greg Blake. "Look, keep the money. Sweet won't need it where he's going. Just don't go through with that hit!"

"I'll think about it," Greg hissed.

"Tell Claudette and Diane I said 'hello'."

Ezekiel backed out of the door. As soon as both feet hit the pavement, he spun around on his heels and sprinted off.

Greg grabbed the photo album and hurled it into the wall in front of him. Photos and illustrations rained down onto the floor of the tattoo parlor in a storm of papyrus and ink.

CHAPTER THIRTY

The steel gate slammed behind him. A welcome sound. Familiar, yet distant, like the last remembered words of a childhood friend.

Sweet was free. The Boss of Bosses was back to rule his streets. His city.

The cream-colored Rolls Royce Phantom pulled up before him. Norm met Sweet with a broad smile as he hopped out of the car and opened the rear door.

Sweet embraced the giant. "Good to see you, Norm!"

"Better to see you...free from *that* bloody Eartha-hole!"

Sweet slid into the Phantom's backseat. He threw his head back and closed his eyes, enjoying the coolness of the soft, leather interior on his skin.

"How have you been, Sweet?" Norm asked.

"I've been incarcerated, *that's* how I've been," Sweet replied. "Any word on Caleb's snitching ass?"

"He's been lying low at home," Norm answered. "There's some other bloke staying there, too. He looks like he could be related to Lydia."

"Mm, Lydia," Sweet sighed. He licked his lips lewdly. "After Caleb is erased, I plan to make up for lost time with her. I got plans for her son, too."

"Oh, yeah? What kind of plans?"

"I'm gonna make him my protégé," Sweet replied. "Gonna take him under my fucking wing!"

"Each one, teach one," Norm said.

"You're goddamned right!"

The Phantom filled with sardonic laughter as it raced through the city streets.

CHAPTER THIRTY-ONE

"What the fuck do you mean, Greg Blake has disappeared?"

Sweet grabbed a fistful of coconut-flavored licorice and gnawed at the bundle.

Norm stood in the doorway, shaking his head. "I called Greg to confirm the hit on Caleb. I got no answer, so I went by his shop. The fuckin' shop had a 'closed for repairs' sign on it. I went by his house...the bloody house was vacant!"

"So, that motherfucker took my money and ran?" Sweet spat.

"It's like somebody tipped him off, or something," Norm

replied.

"Damn! I tell you what," Sweet began. "Call Lala!" He rolled his eyes. "Damn, I hate fucking with that crazy broad!"

"We're gonna kill her after she's done the job, anyway, so don't worry about it."

"True. Make sure she gets it done within the week."

"I'm on it!"

Norm turned and walked out of the office, leaving Sweet alone with his anger.

The Boss of Bosses slammed his fist onto his desk and then took another bite of the coconut confection held firmly within it.

CHAPTER THIRTY-TWO

Lala didn't care that there was a chill in the afternoon air; she just loved ice cream cones.

"It's the sensuality of it," she thought as she spiraled her tongue around the chocolate tip, licking the point down to a sweet, smooth knob.

Lala slid her lips down the ice cream until her full lips touched the cone and then she slowly slid her lips back up, swirling her tongue along the way. The sensation gave her a chill at the base of her spine.

223

Suddenly, she felt another sensation – one that also chilled her – a sharp blade at her throat. Lala paused for a moment and then resumed enjoying her ice cream cone.

"I'm bloody disappointed."

Lala recognized the Cockney baritone. "Norm," she sighed.

"The legendary Lala," Norm replied. "You're slippin', love. It was too easy to sneak up on your sexy little ass."

Norm kissed Lala on the neck and inhaled. He was rewarded with the scent of vanilla and cinnamon. "I could have slit your throat and you wouldn't have even known who did you."

Lala stopped licking her ice cream. "I'll tell you what I *do* know, Norm," she began. "After you slit my throat, I'd perform field surgery on myself – cauterize and sew up the wound. I still might die, but not before you."

Norm frowned. "What? How's that?"

Suddenly he felt it. Something sharp, biting into his inner thigh. He looked down. Between his legs was a knife. Lala held the hilt of the dagger in her free hand.

"Femoral artery laceration," Lala replied. "You'll bleed out in about eleven seconds. Still disappointed?"

Norm removed the knife from Lala's throat and sheathed it. Lala followed suit.

"Not at all, love," Norm replied. "The money has already been wired to your account."

Norm handed Lala a manila folder. "All that you need on the mark is in there."

"Thanks, Norm," Lala said. "Tell Sweet it'll be done by tomorrow night."

225

"Will *do*," Norm replied. "Alligator, love."

Norm turned around and trotted to his SUV.

Lala opened the folder and perused its contents. Her eyes grew wide and her mouth went slack. "Oh, no! Oh, God! What have you done, Caleb? What have you done?"

CHAPTER THIRTY-THREE

With shaky fingers, Ezekiel tapped the doorbell. After a moment, he turned to leave.

The door creaked open and his heart jumped.

"Jason?" Lydia's voice came from behind him. "Did you ring the bell?"

Ezekiel turned to face Lydia, who met him with a broad smile. "I thought you may have walked to the corner store, or something."

"No, I've been at home all

day," Lydia replied.

"Is Caleb home?" Ezekiel asked.

"No, he stepped out for a few hours," Lydia said. "Is there anything I can help you with?"

"Actually, I umm...I came to help *you*."

"Help me? What do you mean?"

"May I come in?"

"Of course. Come on in."

Lydia turned and walked back toward the living room. Ezekiel followed her. Lydia sat down on the couch and held up a book. "I was just reading," Lydia said.

The cover of the book featured two werewolves, locked in a sensual embrace. The male werewolf stood behind the female werewolf. His arms were wrapped around her waist, with his hands on her belly. The female werewolf's hands were resting on the males. They appeared to be enjoying each other's company. Ezekiel knew the book well.

"Immortal II," he said, sounding out each syllable as if he was seeing the book for the first time. "Is it a good read?"

"One of the best," Lydia replied. "Valjeanne Jeffers is one of my favorite authors."

"What genre?"

"Horror and fantasy, with a touch of the erotic."

"Is the author a sister?" Ezekiel asked.

"Yes, she's black," Lydia chuckled. "Why do you ask?"

"My mother was a huge fan of fantasy, horror and fiction written by black authors," Ezekiel replied. "Sword and Soul…Soul and Space…Slashers and Soul…Soul and Steam…"

"Wow, that's a lot of soul,"

Lydia giggled.

"My father used to say that she 'souled' out," Ezekiel snickered. "He never said it to her face, though."

Lydia laughed. "I guess I did too. I love black speculative fiction...now, back to you *helping* me?"

Ezekiel pulled what appeared to be three plane tickets from his jacket. He extended his arm, holding two of the tickets out toward Lydia. He returned the third one to his pocket. "These are tickets to Monterey, California. One for you and one for Z. I'll give Caleb *his* ticket when he gets home."

Lydia giggled and snatched the tickets from Ezekiel's hand. "Yeah, right. Let me see!"

She examined the tickets – the thin cardstock, the smell of fresh ink, the Fluxe font – the tickets were authentic.

"You and Z need to pack quickly and leave ASAP," Ezekiel said. "Go to your Aunt Ruby's. I'm sure she will be happy to see you."

"Why, Jason?" Lydia asked. Her voice shook a bit and to her, the words felt like fish bones in her throat. "And how do you know my Aunt Ruby?"

"Look, your lives are in danger," Ezekiel replied. "Sweet put a hit out on Caleb. I took care of the assassin he hired, but Sweet *will* send another soon. He may already have."

"Sweet *is* a treacherous bastard," Lydia said. "But kill Caleb? Why?"

"Why do you think Sweet was arrested a couple of weeks ago?" Ezekiel's eyes darted around the room as if he was searching for eavesdroppers hiding in the corners and under the couch. His voice dropped to a whisper. "Caleb snitched on him to the

Feds."

"What? That *would* explain Caleb's dark mood as of late…maybe. I…I don't know…"

"Lydia, you have to get yourself and your son out of here!"

"Stop it, Jason!" Lydia ordered. "Just stop it! You're scaring me!"

Ezekiel closed his eyes and shook his head. He took a deep breath and then he spoke. "When I was six years old, around Christmas-time, my father was in Laos, so he couldn't send any money to us…"

Lydia frowned and sat forward, resting her forearms on her lap. "What? That's…"

"My mother was worried that she wouldn't be able to buy me a gift," Ezekiel continued. "She was desperate. She called a man she couldn't stand, but who was certain to help her out – Danny

Sweet."

A chill rushed through Lydia's body and her skin raised in goose bumps. "What? How do you know this? Z didn't even know. This is his…*our* life! How…?"

"I *knew*," Ezekiel replied. "I hid in the pantry and listened to the conversation when you called him. When Sweet came over, I pretended to be asleep, but I sneaked downstairs and watched you."

Lydia stared at Ezekiel in disbelief. "Why do you keep saying 'I', as if you and Z were…?"

"Sweet gave you the money," Ezekiel said. "You promised to give it back, but Sweet said not to worry about it. Then, he grabbed you and tried to kiss you."

"No," Lydia whispered. Shock had kidnapped her tongue and was holding it for high ransom.

"You pushed him away," Ezekiel said. "Sweet laughed...said that one day, you'd wake up, realize you made a mistake in picking Dad and then you'd come running to him."

"Impossible!" Lydia shouted. "What are you saying, Jason, that you...that you're my..."

"Your son. Yes, I am."

Lydia sprang from her seat and stumbled backward into the wall. She wrapped her arms around herself and stood, trembling, as she stared into the eyes of a man half a decade older than her, yet claiming to be her son.

Most frightening was that – in searching Ezekiel's eyes – she found only truth.

"A mother knows her son," Ezekiel said. "I am Ezekiel Octavius Cross, son of Lydia Janae Cross and Caleb Delaney Cross."

Lydia clutched her belly and looked down at her womb, in which she felt a pulsing she had not experienced in fifteen years. The feeling calmed her. In her calm, came clarity.

Lydia looked up at Ezekiel with gentle, loving, tear-filled eyes. "My...son. I..."

Suddenly, Z burst into the living room. "Mom, I just beat Changa's..." Z noticed the tears running down his mother's cheeks and those welling from his mentor's eyes. "Mom...Mr. Locke...is everything okay?"

Lydia glanced at Ezekiel. He shook his head. Z was not ready to hear the truth...to know he was staring his adult self in the face.

"Everything's fine, baby," Lydia said. "Jason just gave us three tickets to visit Aunt Ruby! We could use a vacation, right?"

"Yeah, but why?" Z asked.

"You all have been good to me," Ezekiel replied. "I wanted to repay you."

"Oh, okay," Z said, shrugging his shoulders. "If you say so, Mr. Locke, but what about school?"

"I say so," Ezekiel replied. "You'll only miss a couple of days from school. Everything will be fine. Just trust me, okay?"

"We *do* trust you, umm...*Jason*," Lydia said. "Don't we, Z?"

"I don't see why we shouldn't," Z replied. "Mr. Locke, you're like a father, sensei, big brother, and favorite uncle all rolled into one!"

"Thanks," Ezekiel said. "Gather your things. I'll drive you to the airport and I'll make sure Caleb gets to the airport safely as well."

"I know you will," Lydia said.

She wrapped her arms around

236

Ezekiel's back and brought her lips close to his ear. "I don't know if what you say is true, or if you're stark, raving mad; but I do know that my husband – and we – are in danger, so I will except your help..." She smiled and whispered, "Son," and then she embraced him in silence.

Lydia released Ezekiel and then sprinted up the stairs behind Z.

Ezekiel slumped down onto the couch and – for the first time since the death of his father – cried nearly thirty years of unshed tears.

CHAPTER THIRTY-FOUR

Ezekiel loaded the .45 bullets into a magazine. Half a dozen fully loaded clips were stacked neatly on the coffee table and one was already loaded into his pistol, which rested on the loveseat next to him.

As Ezekiel loaded the last round into the magazine, Caleb burst through the door and stormed into the sitting room.

Ezekiel calmly sat the magazine onto the table and then braced himself for his father's attack.

Caleb snatched Ezekiel up from the loveseat and slammed him into the wall. "Tell me, Jason, why in the hell did my wife call me and tell me that she and my son are at the goddamned airport, headed to California, huh?"

Caleb slammed Ezekiel into the wall again. Ezekiel let his arms hang passively at his sides. "And why in the hell were you the one who bought them the goddamned tickets?"

"Their life is in danger," Ezekiel replied. "Sweet has a hit on you."

"You don't know shit about that, Jason!"

"I know *everything* about it," Ezekiel said. "I know you snitched on Sweet, I know he was arrested because of it, I know Sweet put a bounty on your head."

"Who the hell *are* you, Jason?" Caleb queried.

"You wouldn't believe me if I told you," Ezekiel replied. "Hell, *I* barely believe myself."

"Try me!" Caleb shouted, shaking Ezekiel by his collar.

"I'm your son," Ezekiel said, staring at the olive green linoleum on the floor. "My real name is Ezekiel Cross."

Caleb released his hold on Ezekiel's shirt and shambled backward a few steps.

"You're insane," Caleb sighed. "I let a psychopath into my home."

"I was set up by Sweet, in the future, and sent back almost thirty years into the past in an experiment in time travel."

"Shut up, Jason — or whatever your name is — and get out of my house."

"I don't know exactly *how* we ended up together, but I understand *why*."

"Shut the fuck up," Caleb spat. "And get the hell out of my house!"

He leaped toward Ezekiel, throwing a flurry of quick, fierce punches to Ezekiel's torso and face.

Ezekiel sidestepped, parrying and dodging the powerful strikes.

One punch sneaked past Ezekiel's defenses, however, and connected with his jaw.

Ezekiel stumbled back, shaking his head to exorcise the encroaching dizziness.

Caleb seized Ezekiel's neck. His fingers dug into the soft

flesh, constricting the arteries.

Ezekiel kept his hands at his sides, refusing to fight his father.

He would not even try to escape Caleb's grasp because to escape was to, instinctively, kill.

Suddenly, the doorbell rang.

Caleb released his grip on Ezekiel's neck.

"Saved by the bell, literally," Caleb whispered.

Ezekiel grabbed his pistol from the loveseat and racked the slide. "You strapped?"

Caleb nodded.

"Good," Ezekiel whispered. "I'll answer the door. You cover me."

Caleb lifted his shirt and drew his pistol from its holster. "Let's go."

The doorbell rang again. Ezekiel bounded up the stairs from the basement. Caleb followed behind, swiftly and silently.

"Who's there?" Ezekiel called as he scurried to the door.

Caleb hid behind a wall and aimed his pistol over Ezekiel's shoulder.

"Open the door, big head! It's me!"

Ezekiel and Caleb both breathed a sigh of relief as they recognized Tammy's playful, husky voice.

Ezekiel holstered his weapon and then opened the door.

Tammy jumped into his arms, kissed him passionately for a few moments and then – without words – ran to Caleb and embraced him tightly. Caleb returned the hug and Tammy held on for a long while.

Caleb stared at Ezekiel, who

just shrugged his shoulders and shook his head.

"Tammy, are you okay?" Caleb asked.

Tammy released her embrace and then took a step back. She studied Caleb's eyes for a moment and then turned to Ezekiel. "Can we talk?"

"Of course," Ezekiel said, approaching her.

Tammy took Ezekiel's hand and pulled him toward the kitchen.

Ezekiel stopped and looked over his shoulder at his father. "Lydia and Z are waiting for you. Are you going?"

Caleb stared at the floor. He inhaled deeply, looked up at Ezekiel and then nodded.

"Your ticket is in the living room, under the chess set," Ezekiel said.

Caleb nodded again.

Tammy pulled Ezekiel into the kitchen and then out the back door and onto the deck.

"What's up, Tammy?" Ezekiel asked.

"Will you go away with me?" she asked.

Ezekiel grabbed both of Tammy's hands and gently massaged her fingers with his thumbs. "Baby, are you okay?"

"I love you, Jason," Tammy replied. "Will you go away with me? Right *now*?"

"Slow down, Tammy," Ezekiel said. "What the hell is going on?"

Tammy stared into Ezekiel's eyes as if searching his pupils for some ancient truth. "I love you. Do you love me?"

"I care about you a lot, Tammy. What's...?"

A dark shadow washed over

Tammy's face. Her cheerful, beautiful countenance became, suddenly, hard. "*Care* about me?"

Tammy squirmed her hands free of Ezekiel's and then stared over her shoulder at nothing, at *everything*, at anything other than Ezekiel's eyes. Those eyes she had, moments ago, searched for truth and had gotten it – brutally.

"Look, Tammy, this is not a good time," Ezekiel said. "I can't go anywhere right now. I…"

"Shut up, Jason!" Tammy shouted, interrupting him. "You know what? Forget it! Naw, naw…*fuck* it! I've got a job to do, anyway."

Tammy turned away from Ezekiel and walked back toward the entrance to the kitchen.

Ezekiel grabbed Tammy's wrist and gently pulled her to him. "Tammy…"

Tammy snatched her arm from

Ezekiel's grasp. "It's Lala, nigga!"

The words made Ezekiel jump.

Tammy's face seemed not quite her own. Her voice, somehow...different.

Ezekiel took a step backward. "Lala? *The* Lala?"

"The one and only," she replied.

"It's *you*, then," Ezekiel sighed. "Sweet hired you to kill Caleb."

Tammy gave Ezekiel a quick, pained glance and then headed for the kitchen door.

Ezekiel grabbed her around the waist and pushed Tammy away from the door.

"I am not letting you back in that house!" Ezekiel said as he stepped between Tammy and the entrance.

Tammy drew two Gerber Mark II

fighting knives from the inner sleeves of her jacket. The knives were double-edged, spear-pointed, wasp-waisted blades with pearl handles. She pointed the tips of the wicked-looking weapons at Ezekiel's face as she bent her knees slightly, assuming a knife fighter's posture. "I don't think you can stop me!"

Tammy exploded forward, slashing and thrusting with ferocity.

Ezekiel dodged the whirling blades, shifting from side to side and pivoting around Tammy to keep her off balance.

Tammy drove a kick into Ezekiel's torso. Her heel slammed into his liver, driving him backward in pain.

Ezekiel slammed into the deck's railing. The wood creaked under his weight. Ezekiel shook of the radiating pain in his gut and sprang forward, hammering the side of his head into Tammy's right breast, just below her collarbone.

Tammy's right arm collapsed, flopping, lifelessly, at her side. The Gerber Mark II slid from her fingers and bounced on the deck floor.

Ezekiel grabbed Tammy's left arm and twisted her wrist outward at a painful angle.

The lady-assassin somersaulted sideways, reversing Ezekiel's hold on her wrist. She then leaped upward, driving her knee into Ezekiel's exposed triceps.

Ezekiel snatched his arm away as a sharp pain shot up his arm and into his neck. He shifted to face Tammy, determined to finish her before she systematically tore him apart.

To his surprise, Tammy just stood there, studying him, with tears pouring down her face.

"Why are you fighting so hard

to protect Caleb, Jason?" she
asked.

Ezekiel relaxed his posture,
but continued to focus on Tammy's
eyes. "Because, he's…my father."

Tammy's eyes widened. Her
grip on the knife in her left hand
went slack. "Your what?"

"My father," Ezekiel
repeated. "Sounds insane, I know.
I'm from twenty-seven years in the
future. I was sent here as a test
subject in an experiment in time
travel."

"Then you're…Z?"

"Yes."

"I must be as crazy as they
say, or love really *is* blind,
because…I believe you."

Tammy picked up her knife
from the floor of the deck and
then sheathed both blades in her
sleeves.

Ezekiel sat down on the

deck's steps, massaging his aching arm. He winced as the muscles around the area of his liver spasmed.

Tammy slammed her shoulder against the railing. She screamed as her dislocated arm snapped back into place.

As the pain subsided, she looked down at Ezekiel. He was staring up at her. Tammy felt as if she was staring into a mirror, gazing at the reflection of her hurt; her hope.

"Do you feel *any*thing for me?" she asked.

"Baby, if I wasn't holding on to some small hope of returning to *my* present, I'd follow what my heart wants and allow myself to fall head-over-heels in love with you."

"But, how can you possibly return to the future?"

"Sweet has my watch in his possession," Ezekiel answered.

"That watch is actually a tracking beacon of sorts. It can be used to bring me back home."

"Then let's kill two birds with one stone," Tammy said as she sat beside him. "Let's go get that watch and kill Sweet in the process. It's the only way we can protect Caleb."

Ezekiel nodded in agreement as he stood up. "Let's go!"

"What about Caleb?" Tammy asked.

"He's meeting Lydia at the airport. Going somewhere safe…at least, for a while."

Ezekiel and Tammy sprinted around the front of the house, toward Tammy's Dodge Charger.

"Give me your keys," Ezekiel said. "I'll drive."

Tammy placed her keys in Ezekiel's palm. As he turned toward the car, Tammy grabbed his fingers, stopping him. "You know

I wasn't really going to kill Caleb, right?"

"Yeah, you were," Ezekiel replied with a smirk.

"No, I wasn't," Tammy said. She paused for a moment and then smiled. "Yeah, I was, but only because you hurt me. I needed to vent."

"By killing your best friend? I can think of better ways to deal with pain."

"That doesn't involve killing someone, or sex?"

Ezekiel's brow furrowed as he contemplated Tammy's question. "Touché," he replied, as he hopped behind the wheel of the Charger.

Tammy giggled, hopped into the passenger seat and – triumphantly – slid her seatbelt across her still aching breast.

CHAPTER THIRTY-FIVE

The lobby of Sweet South Records was quiet.

The two security guards on duty sat behind a huge, semi-circular work station, watching the parking lot and outer perimeter on their closed-circuit camera console.

Roger, the elder of the two men, pointed at the monitor. Nine small frames of activity – one frame for each camera – were on the screen.

"Bring up Camera One," Roger

said.

Jerome, the younger guard, pressed a button on the console with a thick, sausage-like index finger. The parking lot popped up on the monitor's screen.

An orange Dodge Charger, with a black racing stripe running the length of its hood, backed into the space next to a silver Chrysler 300.

"Hmm, they're parking next to Detective McGraw's vehicle," Jerome said, shaking his head. "I know they see that 'Reserved' sign."

Tammy stepped out of the car.

"Damn," Roger said, admiring Tammy's body. "She's wearing the *hell* out of those ninja-looking pants!"

"Those are worn by Special-Ops," Jerome said. "The SEALs would wear them all the time down in San Diego when I was in the Navy."

"I thought you were a SEAL," Roger replied.

"No, sir," Jerome said. "I was a 'SWICK' - Special Warfare Combatant Craft Crewman - not a SEAL."

"Well excuse me," Roger replied. "But, never forget, Rangers lead the way."

Tammy sauntered into the lobby.

"How can we help you, ma'am?" Roger asked, approaching her.

"I'm looking for a sexy man who says he works here," Tammy replied. "We met the other night."

"What about the guy who drove you here?" Jerome asked, pointing at Tammy's car on the monitor.

"That's just a guy who *wishes* he could handle all of this," Tammy said, rubbing her firm rear-end.

The security guards ogled Tammy's tantalizing body as she stood before them with her hands on her hips.

"You know, your friend parked in…"

The first thrust severed his vocal cords, so Roger was unable to scream as the second thrust of Tammy's blades speared his armpits and impaled his lungs.

Gurgling sounds escaped the hole in Roger's throat as he drowned in his own blood.

"What the fuck!" Jerome shouted as he drew his pistol.

Tammy slashed furiously with both blades.

The gun fell to the floor. Jerome's severed hands still held it. His sausage-like index finger twitched as if still trying to fire the weapon.

The security guard slumped back into his chair, shuddered

violently for a moment and then lay still. Blood poured from Jerome's arms, forming a slick puddle at his feet.

Tammy opened the lobby doors and waved her hand high above her head, signaling Ezekiel to enter the building.

Ezekiel hopped out of Tammy's car and sprinted toward the Sweet South Records building.

He entered the lobby and paused as he studied Tammy's handiwork. "Fast, efficient, with a little work you..."

"A little work?" Tammy snickered. "Boy, you ain't seen *nothin'* yet!"

Tammy picked up Roger's gun and offered it to Ezekiel. "Here, now you can go in blazing with two guns."

"No," Ezekiel said, waving his hand as if the gun was a fly he was shooing away. "No guns. We do this quietly. Don't want to alert Sweet and give him time to bail."

"Yeah," Tammy replied. "Don't wanna alert the Feds watching this place either."

"Agreed. Let's go!"

Ezekiel and Tammy approached the elevators slowly, steeling their nerves and preparing their minds for what they would meet on the top floor.

CHAPTER THIRTY-SIX

The elevator door opened. Ezekiel stepped off and Tammy followed him. He walked down the hall and stepped through the doors at the end of it.

Sweet's Administrative Assistant – Wendy Dubois – greeted the couple with a beaming smile, which matched her spotless, white business suit. "Welcome to Sweet South Records!"

"Hola, Ms. Thang!" Tammy replied.

Wendy's brow furrowed, but she maintained her smile. "Umm, security didn't call and let me know you were coming up. Do you have an appointment?"

"Girl, naw," Tammy said, waving her hand. "We're just gonna kill Sweet real quick and then we'll be out of your hair."

Wendy bolted upright in her chair. "You – you what?"

Two lightning-fast flicks of Tammy's left wrist and Wendy was spurting blood from both sides of her neck. She instinctively clutched at her throat for a moment, trying, futilely, to halt the torrent of blood. Seconds later, Wendy's head fell back and her eyes went dull.

Ezekiel walked past Wendy's desk to the silver door behind it.

"Wait," Tammy whispered.

"What is it?" Ezekiel inquired.

Tammy grabbed a pen from Wendy's desk and held it out toward him. "You forgot to sign in."

Ezekiel rolled his eyes and then opened the door to Sweet's office.

Lala darted inside. Ezekiel closed the door behind them and quickly surveyed the voluminous room. Sweet sat at his desk, facing the door. Nigerian Norm and Detective McGraw sat on a white, leather couch to Sweet's right.

Ezekiel observed that, although the office was immense, it was not even half the size Sweet's office would be in ten years. And, thankfully, not even a tenth as much security. The security present, however, could not be more formidable.

"Lala?" Sweet said, confused. "What are you...?"

Norm sprang to his feet. "Get Sweet out of here!" he shouted at McGraw. "Now!"

The man-mountain darted forward, slamming his forearms into Tammy and Ezekiel's torsos.

Ezekiel felt as if a cannonball had torn through his guts. The force of the blow sent him flying out the door. Tammy soared through the air beside him.

In mid-flight, Ezekiel spotted McGraw and Sweet speed

past him.

The couple landed in the reception area.

Ezekiel sprang to his feet as Tammy rolled backward into a kneeling fighting posture.

"Don't let Sweet get away!" Ezekiel shouted as he peered over his shoulder at Tammy. "But do *not* kill him. He's mine!"

"So demanding," Tammy said as she scooted toward the exit. "Okay, I won't kill him, but you owe me *big* time!"

Norm drew his pistol. Ezekiel drew his.

"This is going to get noisy," Ezekiel said. "Might draw the feds."

Norm answered with a shrug and raised his weapon.

Tammy scurried down the hall toward the elevators.

Ezekiel ran in the opposite

direction, firing his weapon as he evaded a hail of gunfire, which penetrated the white, brick walls, causing them to vomit clouds of alabaster dust.

****

Tammy reeled backward from the force of the kick. Her torso now bore the giant print of McGraw's shoe.

"You kick like a little bitch!" Tammy said, brushing the dirt from McGraw's size twenty-two shoe off of her chest. "Tae Kwon Do, huh?"

McGraw shook his head. "Yoshinkan."

"Karate?" Tammy snickered. "That's *so* nineteen eighty-five."

McGraw laughed. "So, you're the legendary Lala."

"That's me," Tammy sang.

"Damn, I'm disappointed," McGraw said. "A feared assassin...nothing, but another smart-mouthed hoe with a big booty."

Tammy drew two new Gerber Mark II knives from inside her jacket. "I *do* have a smart mouth, and I do have a pretty big booty, but a hoe?" Tammy twirled the blades around in her hands with lightning speed. "See, now I gots to *cut* ya'!"

McGraw pushed Sweet further down the hallway and then drew his pistol.

Tammy sprang forward, her twirling blades whistling as she moved.

McGraw fired twice at Tammy's head, but the assassin was no longer in his sights. The bullets whizzed down the hallway.

Tammy drove her knife upward, into McGraw's forearm.

The detective howled as the

blade ripped through skin and muscle and skin again. The tip of the knife jutted from the sleeve of McGraw's blazer.

His gun fell to the floor.

Tammy kicked it down the hallway and then, with a sharp twist, yanked the knife from McGraw's forearm, tearing even more flesh upon withdrawal.

McGraw lurched forward, driving his forehead downward. The blow struck Tammy's face with the force of a jackhammer.

Her nose collapsed and shifted off-center. Blood sprayed from her nostrils, polka-dotting her chin and her jacket in crimson.

The two combatants fell to the floor. Tammy, on her back; McGraw, on his rear-end.

The giant detective struggled to pull his sinewy, seven-foot, six-inch frame to a squatting position and then leap-frogged toward Tammy.

Tammy opened her legs.

McGraw landed between them.

Tammy crossed her ankles behind McGraw's back and squeezed with her thighs, trapping him.

McGraw grabbed her throat with his still-functioning hand and squeezed, cutting off the air to her lungs and the oxygen-carrying blood to her brain.

Tammy kicked her feet away from her, driving McGraw backward and his hands from her throat. She then tossed McGraw's dead arm across her chest.

The detective fell forward, his chest collapsing onto Tammy's.

Tammy shifted and threw her left leg behind McGraw's neck, pressing his head down with her muscular calf. She then threw her right leg over her left shin and squeezed with both her knees.

McGraw fought to free himself from the tremendous pressure on his neck, but every movement seemed to lock the choke on tighter.

The giant struggled desperately, but could not escape the boa-constrictor like grip around his neck.

Tammy thrust her knives repeatedly into the top of McGraw's head as she continued to squeeze with her legs.

McGraw's struggling grew weaker until, finally, his body went limp.

Tammy pushed the giant off of her and turned her attention to Sweet. But…there was no Sweet.

Obviously, the Boss of Bosses had tip-toed off during the fight. He was gone. So was McGraw's pistol.

"Damn," Tammy sighed. "My baby is gonna be pissed!"

* * * *

Ezekiel moved deftly from shadow to shadow; appearing just long enough for Norm to spot him and then disappearing again right before the Nigerian giant fired his weapon.

Soon, Norm had spent all of his ammunition, as Ezekiel had done a few minutes before him.

"A Shadow-Strider," Norm said, stepping from behind the cover and concealment of a brick wall. "You must be a student of Chagga Mutwa. Did *he* send you?"

Ezekiel remained silent.

"Alright then, mate," Norm said. "I'm all out of ammo and I'm guessin' you are too, or you would have put a hole in me loaf already."

Norm tossed his pistol into a

corner. "Why don't you come on out and let's have a read…just with our two rubber bands and plates." Norm raised his hands and then pointed down at his feet for emphasis. "I John Major the end result'll be the same as if we blew each other's brains out, ay? So, how about it, then?"

Ezekiel stepped out of the shadows and sauntered to the center of the reception area.

Norm smiled and approached Ezekiel slowly. "I figure you're the bloke that put me mate, Frankie, and his boys to bo-peep. But this ain't just about the bees. This seems personal. I gotta know before I kill ya'…who the bloody hell *are* you?"

"I'm the Ghost of Christmas Future," Ezekiel replied.

"Okay, I guess I won't be killin' ya' quickly, then," Norm said. "Gotta torture ya' first to find out what I wanna know."

Norm rushed forward.

Ezekiel leaped to meet Norm – the Nigerian Giant, the Oxford Assassin, the Cambridge Killer. Ezekiel's master in the arts of murder and mayhem.

They had sparred many times and Ezekiel had never beaten him. He had never come close. This, however, was not a sparring match. *This* was combat. One – or both – of them was going to die. Ezekiel was going to do his damndest to ensure that Nigerian Norm would end up the one permanently on the floor.

Ezekiel struck with a quick combination of two straight punches and a powerful round-kick.

Norm parried the punches, effortlessly guiding them past his shoulders.

The kick, however, crashed into Norm's thigh, sending the giant stumbling sideways.

Ezekiel pounced onto Norm's

back and wrapped a muscular arm around the giant's neck.

Norm grabbed Ezekiel's arms and then forcefully torqued his hips while stepping backward.

The force of the giant's movement sent Ezekiel flying over Norm's shoulder.

He landed flat on his back. The wind rushed from his lungs and out of his grimacing mouth.

The Oxford Assassin drove his heel down onto the side of Ezekiel's elbow. The joint went flat as the bones shattered into tiny fragments.

Another stomp destroyed the forearm and another crushed the small bones in Ezekiel's hand.

A final stomp sped towards Ezekiel's agonized mask of a face.

Ezekiel rolled sideways, just barely evading the devastating attack. The white marble floor shook under Norm's heel.

Ezekiel slowed his breathing and pulled his mind away from the torturous pain in his pulverized arm.

Norm charged forward.

Ezekiel flipped up onto his undamaged arm and drove a thrusting side-kick into the same spot on Norm's thigh he had attacked earlier.

Norm winced as the powerful kick hammered into the sensitive bundle of nerves in his massive thigh.

Ezekiel rolled to his feet and skipped forward with a front knee to Norm's groin.

The giant smacked the inside of Ezekiel's leg, redirecting the blow past him.

Ezekiel followed with a crushing rear knee, once again to the same damaged spot on Norm's thigh.

A low groan escaped Norm's

lips as he staggered backward.

Ezekiel exploded forward with a volley of battering kicks. His steely shins, heels, and insteps all hitting their mark – the tender nerve plexus in Nigerian Norm's thigh.

The behemoth wailed as he felt his thigh collapse inward. The thick femur bone split in two and a jagged piece of bone burst through the seam of his trousers. Norm collapsed onto his belly.

With each beat of his heart, a wave of blood jetted from the hole in his pants.

"Severed femoral artery," a familiar voice said from behind Ezekiel. He didn't have to look. It was Tammy.

"Looks like the Jolly Black Giant is a goner," Tammy said with a shrug.

Norm slowly raised his head and stared at Ezekiel. The colossus' face had grown pale and his unfocused eyes rolled around in their sockets like lottery balls in an air mix machine. "Who the hell *are* you?"

"I told you," Ezekiel relied. "I'm the Ghost of Christmas..."

"Fucking wanker!" Norm whispered.

The giant then shut his eyes. Never to open them again.

Ezekiel breathed a sigh of relief. He turned toward Tammy, who frowned as she noticed his arm hanging lifelessly – and at odd angles – at his side.

"Oh, my God, baby," she said. "We have to get that arm taken care of! I have a..."

Tammy's expression shifted from concern to terror. "Baby, look out!"

Ezekiel whirled around and sidestepped. The bullet that would have blown out his brains, instead, ripped into his shoulder.

Both arms lay dead at Ezekiel's side. He stared into the smiling eyes of the shooter. "Sweet!"

"Yep," Sweet replied as he squeezed the trigger a second time.

The bullet hit Ezekiel in the center of his chest.

"No!" Tammy screamed.

Ezekiel collapsed onto his back.

Tammy sprang forward, drawing her knives as she quickly closed on Sweet.

Sweet scurried backward and fired McGraw's pistol again. The bullet struck Tammy in the knee. She fell to the floor, writhing in pain.

Sweet walked past her, chuckling. "I'll get back to you in a minute, Lala, but first, I gotta see to your boyfriend."

"I'm going to kill you, Sweet!" Tammy shouted.

"Nah," Sweet replied, shaking his head.

The Boss of Bosses stood over Ezekiel. He aimed the pistol downward at Ezekiel's forehead. "I'm not going to ask you any questions. Lala is going to tell me all I need to know. I just wanted to get a close look at the ninja who robbed me. You *are* that ninja, right?"

"*That* was a question," Ezekiel said weakly.

Sweet laughed. "I guess it was. You got balls and a sense of humor. I like that. I wish we could chat longer, but I gotta torture your girl and get my money back before I kill her, so…"

Sweet's index finger slowly pressed against the trigger of McGraw's pistol.

The room fell silent. Ezekiel closed his eyes and

awaited the thunderous sound that would mark his end.

The sound came, tearing silence asunder.

Ezekiel's face, however, remained whole.

He opened his eyes, searching for the reason why the bullet had not found its mark. He looked up into Sweet's pained face. Suddenly a viscous spray of blood erupted from the crime boss' mouth.

Sweet dropped his weapon and then collapsed, in a twisted heap, onto the floor. A thin line of white smoke swirled up from a gaping hole in Sweet's back.

Ezekiel looked up again. Standing in the distance was Caleb, holding a sawed off, twelve-gauge shotgun.

Tammy crawled to Ezekiel and cradled his head in her arms. "Baby, we gotta get you out of here."

Ezekiel shook his head. "I'm done, Tammy. You know I am."

"No, baby," Tammy cried. "You aren't gonna die on me! Hang on! I'll fix you up!"

Tammy looked up at Caleb, who was standing over them, fighting back tears. He shook his head.

Ezekiel stared at Caleb. His father's face seemed blurry and the room seemed to have grown dim. "You were supposed to go to the airport."

"I had two hours before my flight," Caleb began. "So I figured I'd pay Sweet a...visit. When I saw the carnage in the lobby, I figured you were here. I didn't expect to find you here, though, Tammy."

"Well, I...umm..." Tammy stuttered.

"You shouldn't have gotten Tammy involved, Ezekiel," Caleb said.

Ezekiel smiled. "You called me Ezekiel. So, you believe me?"

"Yeah," Caleb replied. "As crazy as it sounds, I do."

"Take care of Z," Ezekiel said. "*Younger* Z. Keep me out of trouble. Be there for me."

"I will," Caleb said.

"Promise me!" Ezekiel shouted.

"I promise…son," Caleb replied. "I'll be the father you…*he* needs me to be!"

Suddenly the room was filled with a loud, humming noise.

Ezekiel turned his head toward Sweet's body. A pale blue light glowed brightly under the cuff of Sweet's suit coat.

"The watch," Ezekiel said. "Sweet. The watch!"

Tammy laid Ezekiel's head gently on the floor and then dragged herself to Sweet's corpse.

Tammy snatched the watch from Sweet's wrist and held it tightly to her breast.

Ezekiel extended his hand toward Tammy.

Tammy's body shook as she burst into tears. She gazed into Ezekiel's eyes and shook her head.

"Tammy...the watch!" Ezekiel said.

"I'll see you soon, baby," Tammy replied.

"Tammy...no!" Ezekiel screamed.

"I love you, Ezekiel."

The humming increased ten-fold.

Caleb dropped to his knees beside Ezekiel. He covered his ears in a futile attempt to muffle the agonizing noise.

Tammy curled up in a fetal position, her body convulsing in pain.

The room was bathed in a blinding, white light and then…

Silence.

Caleb looked around the room.

Tammy was gone.

"Ezekiel, are you okay?" he asked.

Silence.

Caleb did not look at his son. He placed his index and middle fingers on Ezekiel's neck.

There was no pulse.

Caleb hung his head and caressed his son's face as he let the tears overtake him.

CHAPTER THIRTY-SEVEN

Z Z handed Caleb Ezekiel's duffle bag.

"This is the last one, Dad," Z said.

"That's the money bag, son," Caleb replied. "Put that in the car."

"Yes, sir."

Lydia walked out of the house. Her cell-phone was clutched in her fist. "Mali just called. She said she's waiting for us outside."

"Okay, then," Caleb replied. "Let's get this show on the road!"

"Disney World, here we come!" Z said. "I sure wish Mr. Locke could be here to go with us."

"Trust me son, he *is* with us," Caleb replied.

"Look at you, getting all spiritual," Lydia chuckled.

"Was Mr. Locke really a hero?" Z asked.

"Definitely, son," Caleb replied. "He gave his life to save mine. To save this *family*."

"I believe he saved himself, too," Lydia said.

"That's what's up!" Z said. "I think I would have done the same thing."

Caleb placed his arm across Z's shoulders and pulled his son close. "I *know* you would, son. I *know* you would."

CHAPTER THIRTY-EIGHT

Ezekiel opened the door and crept inside.

The house was neat. Clean. Quiet.

No sign of 'The Three', as he called them.

Something shifted in the shadows.

Ezekiel snapped his head toward the movement.

Nothing. Only shadow.

Silence.

And then they pounced out of the darkness and onto Ezekiel.

The Three.

Ezekiel slid his fingers into the armpit of the largest one of the trio and...

...tickled her.

"Who's the most ticklish, huh?" Ezekiel asked. "Is it you, Vicky?"

Vicky giggled as she squirmed away from Ezekiel's grasp.

"What about you, Logan?" Ezekiel said as he tickled the boy.

Logan rolled away and then jumped onto the couch, still laughing.

"No...I believe it's Charity!" Ezekiel said, tickling the smallest of the children.

Charity giggled and kicked her little legs wildly.

"Yep, it's Charity!" Ezekiel snickered.

Mali strode into the room. Her warm smile seemed to chase away the shadows. "Vicky," she began. "Take your little brother and sister outside. Daddy needs his rest. He's had a long day."

"Yes, ma'am," Vicky replied. "Come on, y'all. Let's go outside and play!"

"Yay!" Logan and Charity shouted in unison.

The children sprinted out the front door, slamming the door behind them.

Mali opened her arms.

Ezekiel gave her a big hug and then kissed her softly.

"We signed Ravi today," Ezekiel said proudly.

"The neo-soul singer you've been after?" Mali asked.

"Yeah," Ezekiel replied. "I think she is going to be the next big thing."

"Tell me all about it after your bath. I already ran it for you."

"What's the rush? You have a showing at the gallery later?"

"No," Mali replied. "Your parents *and* mine are coming by for dinner. They want to see the grandkids."

"Dad was working with me all day and didn't mention it," Ezekiel said. "Must be mom's doing."

Mali gently nudged her husband toward the stairs. "Ezekiel hurry!"

"Okay, okay," Ezekiel replied. "I'm on it!"

He bounded up the stairs. Mali headed toward the kitchen.

The doorbell rang.

Mali detoured to the door and opened it.

Standing in the doorway was a woman who matched Mali in beauty and – to Mali – seemed strangely familiar.

"Hello? May I help you?" Mali asked.

"Hi, I'm...Lala," Tammy said. She smiled and extended her hand.

Mali shook Tammy's hand cautiously. "Umm...hi, Lala. I'm Mali. So..."

"Oh, sorry," Tammy replied. "I just purchased the house next door and I wanted to stop by and introduce myself. So, umm...hi, neighbor!"

"Welcome to the neighborhood!" Mali said, chuckling.

Tammy pointed to The Three, who were busy chasing each other around the front yard.

"I'm guessing those are yours," she said.

"Yes. They are very...active," Mali replied. "I hope they aren't disturbing you."

"Oh, no, no," Tammy said. "Lala love the kids...and yours are beautiful!"

"Thank you," Mali said.

"They look just like their daddy."

"So, there's a *Mister* Mali! Is *he* home?"

"Yes, but he's indisposed right now," Mali replied. "I'll be sure to tell him to stop by your house and say hello."

"Great!" Tammy said. "I can't wait to meet him!"

GLOSSARY OF COCKNEY RHYMING SLANG

Adam (and Eve) - Believe

Alligator - Later

Bees (and Honey) - Money

Bo-Peep - Sleep

Boutros Gali - Charlie (Cocaine)

Brad Pitt - Shit

Buster Keaton - Meeting

Butcher's (Hook) - Look

Cat (and Mouse) - House

Dickory (Dock) - Clock

Eartha (Kitt) - Shit

Eighteen (Pence) - Sense

Gregory (Peck) - Neck

Heavenly (Bliss) - Kiss

Joe Rook - Crook

John Hop - Cop

John Major - Wager

Lemon Squeezer - Geezer

Lemon Squeezy - Easy

Loaf (of Bread) - Head

Plates (of Meat) - Feet

Read (and Write) - Fight

Rob Roy - Boy

Rubber Bands - Hands

Sighs (and Tears) - Ears

Trouble (and Strife) - Wife

Twist (and Twirl) - Girl

REDEEMER

The Cross Chronicles

Book II:

GLITCH

CHAPTER ONE

Glitch: A minor malfunction, mishap, or technical problem; a snag

The din of raucous laughter echoed throughout the private dining room of *Sayles' Lobster Bar.* "Sweet" Danny Sweet had just told one of his anecdotes, which were always entertaining and, usually, quite funny.

Sweet's charisma and "favorite uncle" demeanor was in stark contrast to his brutality; his ruthlessness. Those same qualities made him one of the most powerful record industry moguls in the world and the most powerful criminal in the Southeastern United States.

Z loved Sweet. When his father was brutally murdered, it was Sweet who stepped in to give him and his mother support; it was Sweet who found the man responsible for his father's death; and it was Sweet who gave him the opportunity – and the will – to kill that man.

Next to Sweet sat the giant, "Nigerian Norm" – the man responsible for Sweet's safety and for Z's training. Norm, too, was a man of contrasts – massively muscled; brutish; a master of murder, mayhem and pain. But he was also a graduate of the prestigious Oxford Law school, well-traveled, fluent in five languages and one of the most formidable attorneys on the planet.

Norm was Z's instructor in the ways of death and, in that role, as all the others he played, he had done exceptionally well. At fifteen years of age, Z was already an experienced and respected assassin-for-hire and was determined to one day be the absolute best.

Z thrust his fork into a mound of spaghetti gamberetto and then twirled it, wrapping the platinum utensil in a cocoon of pasta and shrimp. He shoved the pasta into his mouth, savoring the spicy-sweet flavor.

The smell of stale cigarettes and coffee assaulted Z's nostrils. "McGraw," he whispered.

Homicide Detective Terry McGraw sauntered into the dining room. His thick, brown fingers fumbled with the buttons of his tweed blazer as he approached the dining table. Behind him shuffled a stout, fireplug of a man, his plump belly jiggling with each step.

"McGraw, what's the good word?" Sweet inquired.

"I've got good news, Sweet," McGraw replied, reaching across the table to shake Sweet's hand.

"Good," Sweet said. His eyes shifted to the clammy-skinned, beer-bellied man beside McGraw and then back to the detective. "Who's the J? And why is he at my table?"

"He witnessed the robbery-homicide at Frankie's spot," McGraw answered. "His name's…"

"Chuck Alexander Etheridge," the fireplug of a man said, extending his plump fingers toward Sweet. "But, everyone calls me 'Shakespeare'."

"Okay. Have a seat McGraw," Sweet said, ignoring Shakespeare's hand. "...Spear-Chucker."

The corners of Shakespeare's mouth curled into a weak smile. "That's Shake..."

McGraw placed a hand on Shakespeare's shoulder and shook his head. Shakespeare wisely shut his mouth and both men sat across from Sweet.

"Hey, Norm," McGraw said, nodding toward the giant.

Hey, John Hop," Norm said, leaning forward in his chair. "You had best brought some good Brad Pitt for this Buster Keaton."

McGraw shook his head. "Damn, I've known you for, what? Eleven...twelve years? And I *still* can't understand a friggin' word when you talk that Cockney shit."

"Well, if you cleaned the wax outta your sighs and had any eighteen in your loaf, understandin' me would be lemon squeezy," Norm said.

"It's British Ebonics," Sweet snickered. "You catch on after a while."

Sweet turned his gaze toward Shakespeare. "So, what you got for me, Shake-n-Bake?"

"It's...ahem...well, I was at Frankie's spot when it happened," Shakespeare replied. "It must have been around eleven, because I arrived at my regularly appointed time of ten-fifteen and had already taken my nightly dosage of opiate."

"Opiate?" Sweet cut his eyes toward Detective McGraw.

"H," McGraw answered.

"Oh," Sweet said. "Go on, Salt-Shaker."

"He came out of the darkness," Shakespeare said, with a sweep of his stubby arms. "Swift; silent...like Death, on gossamer wings."

Shakespeare leapt from the table and paced the floor. He hung his head and closed his eyes. "Frankie and his henchmen did not stand a chance. Their guns meant nothing in the face of that creature of wind and shadow.

"And why are you alive to tell the tale?" Z asked.

"He left all of the patrons alive," Shakespeare answered.

"And just what did this bloke look like?" Norm inquired.

"He was tall, but not nearly as tall as you, or Detective McGraw," Shakespeare replied. "He was, perhaps, five-eleven, or six feet. He was athletically built, with short, well-groomed hair and his skin was a smooth caramel..."

"Damn," McGraw shouted, interrupting him. "Did you get the motherfucker's phone number?"

"Absolutely not," Shakespeare said, turning up his nose. "I am...

"Well, it looks like a new player is in town," Sweet cut in. "He might belong to the Carver Twins; they like hiring them gossamer wing, spirit of the wind-type motherfuckers."

"You thinkin' a sit-down?" Norm asked.

"Definitely," Sweet replied.

Sweet raised his glass of cognac and extended it toward Shakespeare. "Good work, Shakespeare!"

A broad smile spread across Shakespeare's face.

Sweet withdrew a money clip from the inner pocket of his sharkskin suit coat and thrust two crisp hundred dollar bills toward Shakespeare. "Here; there's a lot more in it for you if your information leads to us catching this bastard. Now, order yourself some food; it's on me."

Sweet held up a golden brown French fry. "Hey, Norm, tell Shakespeare what you call these in England."

"Chips," Norm said.

"Freakin' chips! Can you believe that?" Sweet asked. "A chip is a thinly sliced, flat piece of potato. Comes in different flavors, like plain – that's my favorite – barbecue; salt and vinegar – we call 'em 'salt and sour' back home; hot; dill pickle – I don't like them shits, though – anyway, *that's* a friggin' chip!"

Sweet snickered as he shook his head. "You English are some weird motherfuckers!"

"First of all, I'm Nigerian," Norm began.

Sweet rolled his eyes. "Here we go..."

"Second of all, no brother would ever call himself 'English', he'd say he's *'British',* and third..."

"Hold that thought," Sweet said, interrupting Norm. "I gotta take a piss."

"You're already takin' *the* piss, aren't ya'?" Norm replied.

"See...weird!" Sweet said.

Shakespeare smiled wider.

Sweet rose from his chair. Norm followed suit.

"I want in on the sit-down," Z said, dropping his fork onto his plate.

Sweet wiped the corners of his mouth with his napkin. "What?"

"I want in on the sit-down, in case the Carvers get froggy," Z replied.

"What the hell do you think me and Norm are gonna be doing there, little nigga?" McGraw spat. "Playing with our dicks? It don't get no better than me and Norm having Sweet's back."

"The Carvers have some tight security and I hear that the twins are pretty dangerous themselves," Z said. "You can use my help."

"You're fifteen, Z," McGraw sighed. "Leave this shit to the big boys."

McGraw turned his gaze toward Sweet. "Little nigga kills two or three motherfuckers and thinks he's Dirty Harry, or some shit!"

Z pointed toward the silver police detective badge, encased in leather, hanging from McGraw's neck. "Without that badge and gun, you're just a really tall asshole who fights like a sissy with bad feet."

Norm slapped the table with his fingertips. Plates rattled as silverware tap-danced against them. "Ezekiel...enough!"

"Yes, Sensei," Z said, lowering his gaze.

"Bloody hell," Norm shouted. "McGraw is your elder, Z. Apologize!"

"Yes, Sensei." Z turned toward McGraw and pressed his palms together with his hands before his chest as if he was about to pray. "Detective McGraw, I apologize. I was wrong."

McGraw smiled warmly. "It's okay, Z. I accept your..."

"You *are* a really tall asshole who fights like a sissy," Z said, cutting McGraw off. "But you *don't* have bad feet."

The room erupted in laughter.

McGraw thrust his middle finger toward Z.

"That's better," Norm said. "Gotta show the geezers their respect."

"Y'all motherfuckers are crazy!" Sweet chuckled. "Look Z, this game's political. If someone your age attends a sit-down, it'll be taken as disrespect. I know your father – God rest his soul – gave you a soldier's heart and Norm is teaching you to kill like a pro, but you gotta be patient."

"The Carver Twins hired Greg Blake to merc my dad," Zeke sighed.

"And they'll pay for that," Sweet said. "Just like Greg Blake did. You'll have your revenge, little man; we just gotta be smart about it."

"Yes, sir," Z said.

Sweet pulled the brim of his homburg over his right eyebrow. "*That's* my boy! Be right back, fellas; nature calls."

CHAPTER TWO

z Danny Sweet forced a smile as he sat across the table from Virginia and Virgil Carver – the notorious Carver Twins – the only threat and obstacle to Sweet's total domination of rap and R&B music in the South and the Southeast.

Norm and Detective McGraw stood, menacingly, at Sweet's back.

Z sat alone in an apartment across the street – one of Sweet's safe-houses – monitoring the closed circuit cameras and microphones that he and Norm had planted in the restaurant the night before.

At the Carver Twins' backs were two men who Z recognized as former Navy Seals, Manny and Steve. The duo had been securing the Twins since Old Man Carver was still alive and running the family business and the twins were in high school.

"This is my favorite spot," Sweet proclaimed, his voice crystal clear in the microphones hidden in the lamps, wall panels and power strips throughout the room. "The food...the ambience...perfect!"

"My husband – God rest his soul – proposed to me here," Virginia Carver said. "Ah, the memories!"

"And I banged my first piece of ass here," Virgil snickered. "In the restroom. Ah, the memories!"

Virginia punched Virgil in the arm. Virgil winced from the pain. "Ow!" he screamed, rubbing his aching bicep.

"Please, forgive my brother," Virginia said. "So, what exactly, did you want to discuss with us? It sounded urgent on the phone."

Sweet took a bite of the steaming, fried catfish that lay on the plate before him. He licked his lips and pointed at the fish with his fork. "That is some good fish!"

Sweet then pointed the fork in the direction of the Carver Twins, shaking it as he spoke. "For ten years, we've been rivals..."

Sweet sucked a piece of fish from

between his teeth and spat it into a napkin. "We first competed on these streets and now, in the music business. Congrats on signing Point Blank, by the way...he's sure to win Best New Artist at the Hip-Hop Awards. Hell, he might even give my boy, Skinz, a run for his money for Best Album."

"Thank you. We'll see," Virginia replied.

"Well, we've been bitter rivals," Sweet continued. "But we've never broken the peace with each other. There has been no violence between our families and we've all grown because of that."

Virgil glanced at his watch and then yawned.

Norm glanced at the young gangster.

Virginia shook her head.

"Look, Sweet," Virgil began. "I've got a date with a certain supermodel talk-show host in a couple of hours, so, if you don't mind..."

"Virgil!" Virginia shouted, as she placed a firm hand on her brother's forearm.

"It's okay, Virginia," Sweet said, struggling to maintain his smile. "You're right, Virgil, I'll get straight to the point."

Sweet took a deep breath. "Two nights ago, someone killed three of my best men. One of them was a Lieutenant. A reliable source describes the killer as some kind of Special Forces, ninja-type motherfucker. Me!"

Virgil shrugged his narrow shoulders. "So, what does that have to do with us?"

Norm stepped to the table. His face twisted into a manifestation of pure rage. "We'd fuckin' like to know if you set it up, you disrespectful little wanker! That's what!"

Virgil pounded his fist on the table. Plates jumped and a few forks fell to the floor. Virgil glared at Sweet, not once acknowledging Norm's presence with his eyes. "I am Co-Boss of the Carver Family,

Sweet! Since when do you allow your Captain to speak to a Boss at a sit-down?"

"Since when does a Co-Boss who rides the coattails of his sister – the real Boss of your family – disrespect the Boss of Bosses?" Sweet spat.

"The Boss of Bosses?" Virginia said, shaking her head. "You go too far, Sweet."

Sweet took another bite of catfish and spoke as he chewed. "Look, we both know that there isn't a Boss in the Southeast who will stand with you against me."

Sweet sprinkled hot sauce on his fish and took another bite. "But, if you have broken the peace, Virginia, the other Bosses will side with me against you. None of them like the idea of a female Boss, anyway. Me? I'm more progressive."

Virginia scooted her chair away from the table and stood up. Virgil rose almost in unison with her.

Manny and Steve stood at the Carver Twins' flanks.

"This sit-down is over, Sweet!" Virginia said.

"Did you order the hit on my boys, Virginia?" Sweet asked.

"Goodbye, Sweet," Virginia said, as she walked away from the table.

The Carver Family sauntered out of the restaurant.

"Fuckin' wankers!" Norm shouted.

"What do we do now, Sweet?" McGraw asked.

Sweet stared out of a large window, which ran from floor to ceiling in a wall near his table. The Carver Twins were hopping into their limousine.

His upper lip curled into a sneer. "We prepare for war."

"You should send Z's crazy, little ass after them," McGraw said.

"The Carvers are too dangerous," Sweet said. "I can't have my little experiment gettin' himself killed."

"Your experiment?" McGraw inquired.

"I'm creating the perfect killer," Sweet replied.

"I thought Norm, here, was the perfect killer," McGraw said, slapping Norm on his massive bicep with the back of his hand.

"Norm is *almost* perfect, but he was a barrister before I showed him his true calling," Sweet said.

McGraw snapped his head toward Norm. The giant was busy eating a serving bowl of Kale salad. "Damn, Norm...I never pictured you wearing a tight ass apron, making espresso and shit."

"That's a bloody *barista*, fool! I was a *barrister*...an attorney."

Sweet and McGraw laughed. Norm went back to devouring his bowl of kale.

"So, how are we handling the twins, Sweet?" McGraw asked.

"We're gonna use an outsider,"

Sweet answered.

"Anyone I know?" McGraw asked.

"Maybe," Sweet replied. "Her name's Lala."

McGraw sat bolt upright in his chair. "Hold up...Lala is real? I thought she was just a friggin' urban legend."

"Oh, she's real," Norm said, looking up from his now half empty bowl. "Real *bonkers!*"

"I heard she took out Preach, the Boss out of Cincinnati," McGraw said. "And his gang, too, without ever firing a single shot. Man, I thought all that was bullshit, though."

"No, that was really Lala," Norm said. "She only uses silent weapons. Knives and crossbows and other Lord of the Rings-type shit. Sweet has used her a few times."

"Yeah, she does good wet-work, but she's fuckin' expensive," Sweet sighed. "And she's crazy as a shithouse rat! I don't like fuckin' with her unless absolutely necessary. Unfortunately, it's necessary. You'll finally get to meet her, McGraw; she should be here any minute."

"Any minute?" McGraw gasped. "What the hell is she...psychic or something? How did she know you'd be giving her this contract?"

"Ever hear of speed-dial, wanker?" Norm asked.

"The second the sit-down went south, I hit Lala up with a text."

A woman sauntered into the dining room, her Dolce and Gabbana mini dress caressing every curve of her sensuous form with each graceful step.

McGraw whistled in admiration as he perused the woman's body from the top of her unkempt, reddish-brown afro, to her teal Gisele shoes.

"Gentlemen," the woman said. She then nodded in McGraw's direction. "Pervert."

"Speak of the devil," Sweet said, taking the woman's hand.

"And the devil appears," Lala said. "So, who are we killin', sugar?"

Sweet kissed the back of her hand and extended his arm toward a chair. Lala took a seat.

"The Carver Twins," Sweet said.

"Okay," Lala said. "Two-fifty...each."

"Five hundred thousand dollars?" Sweet hissed. "Are you fuckin' serious?"

"I'm the World *Serious* of seriousness, baby," Lala replied. "These are two *crime bosses* we're talkin' about, not some mayor or fuckin' police chief!"

"Two hundred each," Sweet said.

"Two-twenty-five," Lala responded.

"Done," Sweet said.

McGraw exploded forward.

Z's eyes widened and he leaned closer to the monitors as he watched McGraw place a knife to Lala's throat.

Sweet lit a stogie and took a few quick puffs.

"McGraw, what the bloody hell are you doin'?" Norm spat.

"I'm disappointed," McGraw said. "The legendary Lala, huh? It was easy to get the ups on your sexy, little ass. I could have slit your throat and you'd have been dead before you knew who did you."

"I'll tell you what I *do* know, Perv," Lala said. "After you slit my throat, I'd try to cauterize and sew up the wound. Hell, it's worth a shot. I still might die, but not before you."

"How's that?" McGraw asked.

McGraw winced. He looked down toward the source of his pain. Lala held the tip of a knife at his inner thigh.

"Femoral artery laceration," Lala said. "You'll bleed out in eleven seconds. Still disappointed?"

McGraw sheathed his knife on his belt. "Not at all."

Tammy slipped hers back in a hidden sheath on the outside of her clutch bag. She then slammed the back of her head into McGraw's groin.

The detective collapsed onto his knees.

Tammy leapt from the chair and darted behind McGraw. She coiled her arms around his neck and squeezed.

McGraw's eyes turned a bright pink as the constriction on his neck grew tighter.

"That'll be another twenty thousand, or the pervert dies," Lala demanded.

Sweet answered with a nod.

Lala released the choke.

McGraw fell onto all fours, struggling to catch his breath.

"I swear to God, McGraw, if you weren't so damned valuable, I'd kill you myself!" Sweet said.

"Alright gents," Lala said, walking toward the door. She nodded toward McGraw, who was now resting on his knees. "Pervert...gotta get home, *The Walking Dead* marathon is coming on and

I love me some Tyreese."

Lala glided out of the dining room.

Z slipped his Sig Sauer nine millimeter pistol into the waistband of his jeans and then tossed the bottom of his t-shirt over it. "Sorry Lala," he whispered as he shut the door to the apartment. "The Carvers are mine!"

CHAPTER THREE

Z strolled down Abernathy Boulevard, past the old men hanging out in front of the West End Mall to ogle scantily clad girls as they passed by; past the men and women selling incense, fragrant oils and books on the Prison Industrial Complex or the Mayan Apocalypse. He strolled past them all, seen, but unnoticed, just as Norm had taught him to be.

Unnoticed, that is, except by one. One who remained unnoticed *and* unseen by all, stepping in and out of shadow as he traced Z's every step.

Z stopped at the door of a three-story office building nestled between a swanky vegetarian restaurant and a natural hair salon. The sign on the door read '*Carver Recording & Film Studios*'.

Z stepped through the door, drawing his pistol from inside his Enyce vest. The pistol's silencer reflected the light from the chandelier which hung over the security desk. He squeezed the trigger twice.

The first guard slumped in his chair. A torrent of blood gushed from a hole in his neck. Within seconds, his starched, white uniform shirt was a deep burgundy.

The second guard collapsed to the floor as blood and tissue erupted from his back. A wisp of smoke rose from the hole in his black security officer's shirt as he convulsed erratically. A moment later, he lay still.

Z sauntered to the elevator, pressed the button and waited.

The elevator door slid open. Z turned his back to the elevator, admiring his handiwork as he stepped into it. The elevator came to a smooth stop on the third floor. The door opened and Z stepped out of it into the hallway. The skylights that ran the length of the hallway's ceiling bathed the corridor in the warmth and light of the noonday sun.

Z perused the numbers on the studio and office doors, stopping at 'Studio 9', from which emanated the din of southern gangster rap music, laughter and firm commands. Z recognized one of the commands belonging to the voice of Virginia Carver. He had found at least one of his targets.

Z raised his pistol before him. He then took half a step back from the door, inhaled deeply and then drove the heel of his foot toward the doorknob.

His heel crashed into the door, just below the knob. The door frame shattered and the door flew open. Z rushed in, squeezing off a volley of rounds from his pistol.

The Carver Twins' bodyguards, Manny and Steve, threw their bodies in front of their bosses, as Z had hoped – he did not want to have to face these two killers *and* the twins – and were caught in a hail storm of searing lead. Round after round tore into their flesh, rending tissue, bone and vital organs. The big men fell, soiling the hardwood flooring with entrails and gore.

The rapper Point Blank dropped to his haunches in the recording booth, thrusting his head between his legs.

Virginia Carver darted forward, closing on Z with fearsome speed and ferocity. Her hands wrapped around his pistol, as she pushed her arms high above her head. A round exploded from the gun, lodging in the ceiling.

Z tried to pull the trigger again, but Virginia held the pistol's slide firmly in place and the gun would not fire.

Virginia jerked the weapon downward.

Z's index finger, caught in the trigger guard, made a sickening snap as it bent sideways at an impossible angle. Z dropped to his knees, releasing the pistol.

Virginia thrust her knee forward, driving the air out of Z's lungs as the powerful knee strike collided with his solar plexus.

Z tried to crawl away, but a heavy, leather boot came crashing down on his left hand, crushing the small bones and pinning it to the floor.

Z screamed in agony as he looked up into Virgil's smiling face.

"Where are you running to, boy?" Virgil snickered. ""Don't you have some killing to do?"

"This is one of Sweet's boys," Virginia said.

She stomped on his right hand, crushing his other fingers.

Z screamed again.

The hammer of Z's pistol clicked as Virginia cocked it. "We're gonna send what's left of your head to Sweet. The rest of you, I'm gonna keep on display in pickle jars in my pool-house."

Virginia aimed the pistol at Z's forehead. A loud boom rocked the studio.

Blood and brain splashed onto Z's face.

A second boom. More blood and brain rained on the floor before the teen.

Z scurried across the floor, slipping in blood and bits of flesh.

The headless bodies of the twins collapsed onto the floor with dull thuds.

Z reached out toward his pistol. With shaky fingers, he snatched it off the floor and raised it toward the entrance. There was no one there.

"Put the gun down, Z."

Z leapt to his feet, aiming his pistol toward the source of the rich, baritone voice. Standing before him was a tall, athletically built man holding a sawed-off 12-gauge shotgun on his shoulder. Although Z had never seen him before, the man looked strangely familiar.

"Who the hell are you?" Z inquired. "How do you know my name?"

"You're welcome," the man replied.

"Thanks," Z said, keeping his gun aimed at the man. "Now, who the hell *are* you?"

"My name's Ezekiel," the man answered. "Ezekiel Cross."

"Bullshit!" Z shouted, struggling to ignore the intense pain gnawing at both hands.

"Naw, boy, that's *real* shit," the man said. "As real as the shock you're gonna go into if we don't get those hands taken care of."

A wave of nausea washed over Z. The pistol fell from his shaky fingers and he collapsed against the mixing board. Ezekiel ran to Z and placed a powerful arm around the boy's waist. "We have to get out of here. I'll explain everything later.

Z nodded. Ezekiel sat Z in a chair and retrieved the boy's gun. He tucked the weapon into the holster sewn into the interior of Z's vest and then helped him to his feet. The duo crept out of the office and into the sunlit hallway.

"I can walk now," Z said.

"You sure?" Ezekiel asked.

"Positive," Z answered.

Ezekiel let him go. Z stood wide-legged, remaining still until he was sure that his balance would not fail him. He then sauntered down the hall toward the elevator with Ezekiel on his heels.

A low *"ding"* came from the elevator and the door slowly slid open.

Ezekiel raised his shotgun, holding it at the ready. Z took a few steps backward until he was standing a couple of feet behind Ezekiel.

An immaculately dressed, elderly man stepped off the elevator and stood before the elevator door, offering only his profile to Z and Ezekiel. The man was tall, but his spiky, grey afro made him appear even taller. His full, grey beard seemed to glow against his mahogany skin and his frame, though covered in a tailored grey suit, was obviously athletic, despite his age.

"Oh, no," Ezekiel gasped.

"What? Who is that?" Z asked.

"He's called Paradox," Ezekiel whispered. "When a time traveler changes history, Paradox comes and fixes it back."

"Man...what? Paradox?" Z said, shaking his head.

"That's *Grandfather* Paradox to you," the elderly man said. "Always respect your elders, boy."

"What do you want, old man?" Z inquired.

"You," Paradox replied. He turned his head slowly toward Z, revealing a wide grin.

Fire erupted from the muzzle of Ezekiel's shotgun.

Paradox was thrown onto his back as a sabot shotgun slug blew a chasm in his chest.

"Run!" Ezekiel shouted.

Z did not move. "Run? You just ghosted that old nigga!"

"Damn, I do *not* recall being *this* stupid!" Ezekiel spat. "Now, we've got to fight this thing."

"Man, I appreciate you saving me and all," Z said, approaching Paradox's body. "But you are straight cray-cray, for real!"

"Cray-cray?" Ezekiel asked.

"That means you take crazy to a whole 'nother level," Z said. If you really believe you're..."

The words grew heavy in Z's throat as he watched Paradox sit up on his haunches.

"The hell?" The teen gasped.

Paradox rose to its feet. It raised its head toward the ceiling and let loose a roar that sent a chill clawing its way up Z's spine. The creature shifted...changed. Tendon, sinew and bone popped and crackled as they changed shape and function. The Grandfather Paradox was no longer a sophisticated, athletic elderly gentleman; it was now gaunt to the point of emaciation, its desiccated skin was pulled tautly over its bones and its complexion was now the pallid, ash-gray of death. Strange runes and raised patterns traversed the creature's flesh. Its eyes were pushed back deep into their sockets, what lips remained were tattered and bloody and the monster gave off a strange and eerie odor of decay and decomposition; of death and destruction; of disease, sickness and shit.

Z whirled about and took off. The Grandfather Paradox exploded forward, sprinting on all fours, hot on Z's heels.

"*Now*, you run?" Ezekiel sighed.

Ezekiel squeezed the trigger of his shotgun.

The creature fell over on its side as its forearm was blown from its elbow.

Ezekiel squeezed the trigger once more. The shotgun roared.

Paradox's head exploded, its oily, black ichor painting the walls and floor.

Z darted out of the emergency door. Ezekiel followed.

"Keep going," Ezekiel shouted. "That thing will be back at us in a few minutes!"

Ezekiel and Z reached the main floor. They ran through the door and into the lobby, continuing on, sprinting past the corpses of the pair of security guards.

"My car is parked around the corner...to your left," Ezekiel said.

The duo ran out of the building and onto Abernathy Boulevard. Almost in unison, they reduced their speed to a brisk walk, so as to not attract too much attention.

"Time travelers...old men turning into monsters...what the hell is *really* going on, shawty?" Z inquired.

"Welcome to *my* world, kid," Ezekiel sighed. "Welcome to my world."

"Your world is jacked up," Z replied. "All hell is gonna break loose out here if that thing spots us out here."

"It won't follow us out here," Ezekiel said. "Paradox spirits exist to set things right when damage is done to the timeline. The two of us existing at the same time is major damage, so the daddy of all Paradoxes showed up. But if it attacks us out here, it puts innocent people at risk – people whose time isn't supposed to be up yet. It would damage the timeline itself

331

and its very nature won't allow it to do that."

"So, we're safe, then," Z replied. "That thing missed its shot, huh?"

"Nope," Ezekiel said. "It'll come after us as soon as it can catch us away from the public eye."

"Great," Z sighed. "Guess I'll be sleeping out on these streets."

The corners of Ezekiel's mouth rose a bit. "You won't have to," he said. "We're gonna kill the Grandfather Paradox. Thanks, for the reminder."

"Huh?" Z said, scratching his head. "Reminder?"

"Yeah, when you mentioned sleeping on these streets," Ezekiel replied. "About twenty years from now, a homeless guy in Chicago is gonna kill a paradox spirit called Wynter."

"You're serious?"

"Yeah," Ezekiel said. "In fact, your boss, Sweet, told me the story. He's fascinated by anything to do with time and time travel."

"I didn't know that," Z said.

"There's a lot about Sweet you don't know, kid," Ezekiel said. "But you'll learn...hopefully sooner than later."

"Tell me about this Wynter spirit," Z said.

"Alright," Ezekiel replied. "I'll tell you what I remember of it."

"See, there was this doctor named...Yemi, I think," Ezekiel said. "She was the assistant to Dr. Kline – that's the nutjob who set me up and sent me here...I'm gonna kill her when I get back home...but anyway...Dr. Yemi...what is her last name...she comes back in time with a piece of tech she and Kline built called a thermophone – figured she'd get filthy rich introducing future tech in the present; maybe even win a Nobel Prize, but doing so caused a powerful paradox spirit to come and set things right. Here's how it went down..."

CHAPTER FOUR

10 Years From Now

"Careful, Dr. Cruz, it's hot! *Nuclear* hot!" Yemi extended her cocoa-toned hand towards Dr. Cruz in warning.

Doctor Cruz placed his thick lips to the rim of the porcelain mug and took a quick sip. "The hotter, the better in this damned deep-freezer you call a laboratory."

"It's going to get much hotter in here in a minute," Yemi said as she smiled, knowingly, at her team. "How's your Chai?"

Doctor Cruz closed his eyes and inhaled deeply. The tea smelled pleasantly of cinnamon, vanilla, honey and cardamom. He took another sip. "Tastes good, I *think*. My taste buds are too cold for adequate critique."

Everyone laughed. Yemi raised her wrist to her face and squinted at the hands of her watch. "Red should be waking up any minute now."

A high pitched, electric chant rose from the storage room at the rear of the lab.

Charles, the electrical engineer on Yemi's team, shook his bald head. "Voodoo Child. It's always Voodoo Child."

Red shambled out of the storage room. His long, kinky locks danced upon his shoulders as he threw back his head in ecstasy and worked his wizardry upon the strings of his guitar. The ivory guitar looked to Yemi like an axe of bone. An axe, wielded by a master woodsman.

"Well, I'll stand up next to a mountain and chop it down with the edge of my hand."

Dr. Cruz pulled at the collar of his sweater. "Is the tea making me so warm?" He said to himself. He looked around the laboratory. Everyone was unzipping their parkas. Dr. Cruz quickly unbuttoned his wool trench-coat. "I'll be damned!"

Yemi smiled and patted Dr. Cruz on the shoulder.

Dr. Cruz stared, wide-eyed, at Red as he sang and continued to play. "You guys have done it!"

The team's thermodynamics expert, Paige, rose from her chair and waved her sinewy arm towards Red's guitar. "Dr. Cruz, we present to you...the Thermophone!" Paige took a deep bow. Everyone applauded. Red bit his bottom lip as he hit a hard-rock double crescendo.

Dr. Cruz joined in the applause. Red slowly opened his eyes. "Warm enough for ya', Doc?"

Dr. Cruz leaped from his seat, wrapped his arms around Red's shoulders and squeezed. "Son, you just made history!" Tears welled up in the corners of his eyes as he stood before the triumphant team. "You *all* have just made history!"

"We couldn't have done it without the financial backing of Cruzcorp." Yemi said.

"Yeah," Red agreed. "Now, maybe Yemi can relax, settle down and have me some babies."

Yemi laughed and shook her head. "We can't raise babies in that storage room, Red."

The lab erupted in laughter.

"Hey, my little condo beats that tent on Lower Wacker I used to call home." Red replied.

"Dr. Cruz's jaw fell slack. "You're homeless, Red?"

Red shook his head. "I refer to my present situation as '*residence*less'. Home is where the heart is."

Yemi rose from her swivel chair. "With your permission, Dr. Cruz, let's continue this demonstration."

"Please, do, Dr...Falana..."

[*"That's* it, *Ezekiel said. "Falana. I knew her last name would come to me!"*

"Come on, bruh," Z replied. "I wanna hear the rest of the story."

"Okay," Ezekiel said. "Back to it..."]

Yemi turned to her audio engineer, Trina, who was sitting at her mixing board. "Trina?"

"The thermophone – as we call it – absorbs externally generated sound, and then transduces the sonic vibrations into heat," Trina began. "The stronger the sonic vibrations – meaning the louder the sound – the greater the heat it generates."

Trina began deftly pushing levers and pressing buttons on the mixing board. A large amplifier, which sat in the corner of the laboratory, popped and hummed. Trina nodded at Red. "The guitar is now calibrated to the amplifier's wireless frequency."

Red climbed up onto a desk, pushed the papers on the desk onto the floor with his feet and assumed a wide-legged stance.

Charles checked the thermometer at his terminal. "The temperature is now sixty-two degrees Fahrenheit," Charles turned a dial beneath the thermometer. "I'm reducing the temperature to fifty degrees Fahrenheit...thirty seven degrees...button up everybody...twenty degrees...six...four below zero...we are now congruent with the external temperature of negative twelve degrees Fahrenheit."

"It's all yours, Red!" Paige yelled.

Red closed his eyes and gently caressed the sleek body of his guitar. "C'mon, Pearline," he whispered seductively.

Red lovingly stroked Pearline's strings until she moaned her approval.

"Whoa," Dr. Cruz quickly unbuttoned his coat and tossed it to the floor. He turned to Yemi, who's removed her parka as she closed her eyes and enjoyed the music. "What is that he's playing, Dr. Falana?"

"Maggot Brain." Yemi replied.

"Strange name for such a beautiful song."

"Not so strange. Put maggots on a wound and they will eat the decay and filth, leaving clean, healthy flesh. This song, played by a master guitarist like Red, does the same for the brain of the listener."

"Interesting. It is quite cathartic. Who came up with such a brilliant idea for a song? Bach? Dylan? John Lennon, perhaps?"

Yemi laughed and shook her head. "George Clinton and Eddie Hazel of Parliament-Funkadelic."

Dr. Cruz turned away from Yemi. His face had turned from dark olive to beet red. "Okay, back to the experiment."

Pearline's moans and lamentations faded to a whisper. Sweat poured from Red's mahogany forehead and down his cheeks. Red leaped from the desk. Yemi rushed to him and snatched the down-filled jacket from around his shoulders.

Charles looked at the thermometer. "Seventy-eight degrees. One more bar and we should reach a hundred degrees."

Red resumed playing "Maggot Brain". Pearline's whispers increased to ecstatic cries.

The room grew very hot.

Dr. Cruz wiped the sweat from his neck with his hand.

Suddenly, Pearline's cries died, as if cold hands had encircled her throat and cruelly squeezed. The track lights popped and the equipment coughed and then...darkness...and silence.

"Damn it! Trina groaned.

"Coats on everyone," Yemi ordered. "The generator should kick-in in just a second and we'll commence with the demonstration."

Minutes ticked by. The temperature plummeted.

"That generator's a no-go," Charles said. "Come on, Paige. Let's go check it out while we still have daylight. More likely than not, the snow knocked a power line down and the generator probably just needs some oil."

Paige slid on her mittens as Charles pushed open the heavy, steel door. A rush of cold wind and snow slapped him in the face. "Let's make this quick," he said. "It's getting nasty out there."

Paige and Charles trudged out into the uncompromising Chicago winter.

***

Heavy flakes of snow and marble-sized hailstones pummeled Paige and Charles as they struggled towards the alley behind the laboratory. A high-pitched whistling pierced the baritone howl of the wind. "What the hell?" Paige said, as she looked skyward towards the conspicuous whistling. Suddenly, a massive, shimmering cube came into view above her.

"Shit," was all she could manage to scream before the immense block of ice crushed her under its tremendous weight. The Buick-sized ice-block hit the ground with a thunderous crack and then exploded into thousands of shards.

Charles was caught in the maelstrom of frozen shrapnel. His flesh shredded like cheese through a grater.

Charles fell to the ground beside the mass of bone and skin that was once Paige. The wind snickered as snow quickly consumed their tattered bodies.

***

What is taking those two so long?" Trina asked.

"Dunno." Red replied, as he plucked the theme from 'Enter the Dragon' on Pearline. The temperature held at a brisk fifty degrees.

"Red," Yemi sighed, as she pointed at his guitar. "The light."

Red examined Pearline. The low-battery indicator flashed blood red. "Damn," he groaned. "We've got ten minutes at best. If Charles and Paige don't get that generator on soon, it's gonna get cold as a witch's tit in here *real* quick!"

Trina yanked her wool cap over her forehead. "I'm going out there. They should be back by now."

Trina pushed the door. It did not budge. She pushed harder. Still, no movement. She placed her back against the door, bent her knees and then burst backward, slamming her weight into the steel door. The door remained defiantly still.

"The door's frozen shut," Trina said. "Gotta go up top."

"Be careful, Trina." Dr. Cruz replied.

"Careful's my middle name."

Trina bolted up the stairs and ran to the French windows on the balcony. The windows were covered in frost. She unlocked a window and snatched it open. "I'm gonna take the fire escape," she yelled, leaning over the balcony railing.

"Okay." Yemi yelled back.

Trina turned back to the window and was met with by a battering-ram of snow, which slammed into her chest and sent her rocketing over the balcony railing.

She hit the floor with a loud thud.

Columns of snow poured over the balcony.

"Madre de Dios!" Dr. Cruz screamed, as he drew a cross on his forehead and torso with his fingers. He stared incredulously as the avalanche continued to pour from the upstairs window and over the balcony.

"Trina!" Red cried, staring at Trina's twitching body, as it disappeared under a mound of reddening snow.

Yemi fell back into her chair. "No. No. *No!*"

Pearline's low-battery indicator flickered and then went dull. The guitar choked out one final note.

"Pearline's dead," Red said. "No spare batteries."

Yemi pulled her cell-phone from her jacket pocket. Her fingers shook as she pressed '9-1-1'.

"Hello? We're at forty-three thirteen west Lake Street...Falana Technologies...there's been an accident...my audio engineer...my friend...is dead."

Tears flooded Yemi's cheeks and exploded as they landed on the armrest of her chair. "She...she fell...Trina Malloy...My name is Efunyemi Falana...Efunyemi Falana, yes...okay, please hurry! Thank you."

"What did they say?" Red asked.

"The streets are covered in ice. There's five feet of snow out there."

"Jesus," Red said, as he hung his head. "It'll take hours."

"Yeah." Yemi's shoulders shook as she began to sob.

Dr. Cruz ran to the door and pushed. He pushed until the color under his nails went from rosy to off-white. "We have to get out of here! If we don't, we'll freeze to death!"

Yemi closed her eyes and rubbed her temples. "Dr. Cruz, calm down. The door is snowed shut. The windows are death traps. Let's huddle together and think this through."

Dr. Cruz slowly turned away from the door. "Yes, of course. You're right. Think this through. Yes."

Red ambled over to his ad hoc condo. "Be right back," he said, as he disappeared into the storage room. He reappeared a minute later with a bundle of newspapers cradled in his arms and several thick, wool blankets over his shoulders.

Red spread one blanket out on the floor and then covered it with the newspapers. He threw another blanket over the newspapers and then sat upon it cross-legged. "Sit here," Red said. "I have blankets for everyone."

Dr. Cruz and Yemi sat close to red and wrapped themselves in blankets.

"Why the newspapers?" Dr. Cruz inquired.

"For insulation," Red replied. "Holds the heat. Old vagabond's trick."

Yemi forced her eyes to look everywhere but the crimson snow-mound in the center of the laboratory. Her gaze caught the thermometer, which read 'nine degrees'.

Dr. Cruz blew his warm breath into his clasped hands and then rubbed his palms together briskly. "C-cold."

Red handed Dr. Cruz and Yemi two large wads of tissue paper each. "Squeeze a wad in each fist, place your hands under your armpits and rub your forearms up and down your chest," Red ordered. "It'll warm you up, some."

Dr. Cruz and Yemi followed Red's instructions. Red craned his head towards Yemi and peered into her eyes. He noticed that Yemi's walnut-brown face was now a blue-brown patchwork. "Hang in there gorgeous."

Yemi forced a smile through the shivers. "We make it out of here...dinner's on me."

"And a movie." Red replied.

A laugh crawled from between Yemi's blue-brown lips. "Sure. I'll even throw in a bucket of popcorn."

"Damn, it's a date, then."

Red, Yemi and Dr. Cruz laughed weakly and huddled closer in the darkening lab.

The thermometer cracked at eighteen degrees below zero.

***

"Christ, what happened here?"

Uniformed police officers cleared a path as the paramedics rushed in with stretchers...and body bags.

A paramedic knelt down beside Red and placed two fingers on his neck. The warmth against Red's cold flesh stirred him. His eyes fluttered open.

"This one's still breathin'! The paramedic shouted.

"Guess there *is* a friggin' God." A police officer responded.

As the paramedics strapped Red onto the stretcher, movement on the balcony caught his eye. If his vocal chords were not constricted from hypothermia, he would have screamed.

On the balcony was what appeared to be a man – or a man-like *thing*. The creature was stark white and dressed in a white, tailed tuxedo and white top-hat.

The man-creature leered down at Red, smiled and then tipped his hat.

Red felt nauseous. The room whirled and dipped. Whirled...and dipped.

The creature kicked his white, spindly legs up like a dancer in a cabaret burlesque. It pirouetted and then disintegrated into delicate flakes of snow.

Red faded into unconsciousness as the wind cackled in his frost-blackened ears.

20 Years From Now

"Red? Red, you there?"

An adolescent boy crawled into the spacious, four-person tent. His corduroy trousers made swishing noises with each movement of his thin legs.

"Red?"

"I'm right here, Stew."

A lantern flickered on, illuminating the tent in dim, white light. Red sat cross-legged at the far end of the tent.

Stew giggled. "Pushups in the dark again, huh?"

"Gotta always be ready son."

"Ready for what?"

Red did not answer. Stew looked around the tent. The walls were lined with prints and photocopies of articles about Chicago blizzards spanning several years, but – in particular – about the blizzard a decade ago, which claimed the lives of hundreds of homeless people – and a team of scientists, along with a billionaire industrialist, who were all involved in some sort of failed project.

"Oh," Stew nodded. "Ready for *him*."

"*It*." Red said.

"But, isn't it still in hibernation? You said..."

"It's been ten years, Stew. Today's the first day of winter. Nap-time's over."

"So, what do we do?"

"*I* destroy the sumbitch. *You* stay your ass away from here until I kill it...or until the first of spring."

Stew shook his head. "I wanna help, Red! I..."

Red pushed upwards with his massive arms and sprung to his feet. "I'm not kiddin', Stew! Old Whitey ain't nothin' to play around with!"

Red drew his guitar from its leather case. "Besides, Pearline is all the help I need."

The tent's door-flap flew open and the tent was flooded with sunlight. Red blew out the lantern.

A woman stuck her head into the tent. To Red, her smile seemed brighter than the imposing sunlight.

"Come on, guys. We have to set up. In about two hours, the lunch crowd will be pouring in." The woman said.

Stew scrambled towards the door-flap. "Coming, mom."

Red slipped his parka on over his safari vest. "I'll be right out, Denise."

Red dipped his hands in and out of a crate in the corner of the tent, snatching out handful after handful of D-batteries, which he quickly stuffed into the many pockets of his vest.

"C'mon, Red!" Stew called.

Red grabbed Pearline and then glided out of the tent. "Ok, let's motivate!"

Denise kissed Red on the cheek. "Morning, Red."

"Morning."

Stew tugged at Red's parka. "So, what are you doing after we close, Red?"

Denise rolled her eyes. "Here we go, again."

"Going home...probably work on some material for tomorrow's performances." Red answered.

Stew smiled slyly. "Mom rented 'Manchurian Candidate'. The Denzel version. I know the Sinatra version is your favorite movie, but *this* one's even better, Red!"

Red shook his head. "Well, if anyone could top 'Old Blue Eyes', it'd be Denzel, but a better movie? I dunno."

"You're welcome to come over, Red," Denise said. "Now, give the matchmaking a rest, Stewart!"

Stew crossed his fingers behind his back and smiled. "Yes, ma'am! Whatever you say."

"I wish I could," Red sighed. "Next time, for sure."

"You're welcome, any time, Red." Denise replied.

The trio trudged along through the snow, past the other homeless citizens of Lower Wacker Drive. Denise hugged and "helloed" everyone that was out and about.

Red snickered as he nudged Denise. "Ever miss it out here?"

"Actually I do, sometimes," Denise answered. "Not enough to make me move back though!"

Red laughed. "I bet. We can't have that, anyway. We need you right where you are."

"Especially me, mom," Stew chimed in. "Without you and Streetwise Café, my game collection would be lame!"

Denise shook her head. "If I could get you to *read* half as much as you play those video games, I would be overjoyed!" Denise pressed a button on her keychain. The doors of her SUV clicked as the locks were opened.

Stew frowned. "If I read *that* much, *my* joy would be *over*!"

Red laughed.

Denise smiled and shook her head. "Get in the truck, Stewart."

Everyone climbed into Denise's vehicle.

Denise crept along Michigan Avenue. Large snowflakes clung to the windshield.

Denise turned on the wipers. "Snow's getting heavier."

Red stared out the passenger window. He felt his heart racing. His throat constricted and his tongue felt thick. It was almost time.

Denise gasped. "What in the world?"

Red snapped his head in Denise's direction. "What's wrong?"

"Some fool in tails is dancing in the middle of the street!"

Red peered through the windshield. About half a block away was Old Whitey, the thing that had taken his friends from him a decade ago. The thing that had taken his home. The thing that he had been waiting for, had been – it seemed – waiting for him also.

Stew peeked over Red's shoulder. "Red is that...?"

"Yeah, son," Red replied. "That's it."

"That's *what*?" Denise asked.

Red threw the hood of his parka over his head. "Stop the car, Denise."

"Why? What's...?"

Red planted a gentle, but firm hand on Denise's arm. "Denise, stop the car!"

Denise veered towards the sidewalk and slowly came to a stop. Red continued to stare at Old Whitey as it danced closer.

Old Whitey's stick-like limbs and angular joints whipped through the crisp air as it performed its ballet on ice.

Denise stared at the creature through the windshield. Her fingers gripped the steering wheel tightly. "Okay, guys, explain. Who *is* that?"

Not 'who'," Red answered. "*What*. The Norsemen called it 'Ymir', the ice giant. When it came to America with the Pilgrims, Native Americans called it 'Winter Katsina'. I call it Old Whitey. It's the thing that murdered my friends and all those hundreds of homeless ten years ago.

"Like Daddy, mom." Stew said.

Old Whitey skipped closer. Denise could now make out it's sharp features. Like a man, but...different.

"My God!" Denise grabbed Red's hand. "What do we do, Red?"

Red undid the latches on Pearline's case. "We're going to get out and head for Grant Park. Stay on my heels!"

Denise shook her head. "Shouldn't we drive? It'd be quicker and the snow is getting worse."

"If you stay in this vehicle, it will become your tomb. That thing will trap you in here, Denise. Now, let's go!"

Red hopped out of the SUV. Denise followed. Stew climbed out of the SUV and ran to his mother's side. Denise tucked Stew's scarf into his jacket and then took his hand.

Pearline began to purr as Red's fingers danced gracefully across her strings as he played a rendition of Screamin' Jay Hawkins' 'I Put a Spell on You'. The snow beneath the trio's feet began to melt into puddles as the song escaped Pearline's internal amplifier. Red increased the volume. A wave of heat emanated from Pearline. Old Whitey grimaced in pain as the searing air struck it. The creature leaped backwards out of Pearline's range.

Stew unzipped his jacket and untied his scarf. Red unzipped his parka. Denise stared at Red as she unbuttoned her coat. "Red, how in the hell are you doing this?"

"It's what we were working on ten years ago," Red replied. "Let's move. Stay close!"

Red trudged on. His fingers did not cease caressing Pearline's strings. An expanse of warm, moist land stood before them, as Pearline cleaved through the ice and snow. The ground behind them, however, was buried under massive mountains of snow.

A short distance away, Grant Park's band shell rose up out of the snowy horizon.

Red yelled over Pearline's cries. "Almost there!"

Stew peered over his shoulder. Old Whitey was on their tails, surfing on a mammoth wave of snow. The creature flashed Stew a wide, crooked grin. Stew snapped his head forward. "It's close, Red! *Real* close!"

"Don't worry, it won't come close enough to harm us. It can't stand the heat." Red replied.

"So, what's the plan, Red?" Denise asked.

"Me and Pearline will keep Old Whitey at bay while you turn on the speaker system at the band shell."

Denise shook her head. "They keep the band shell locked, Red."

"I busted the lock a week ago. Pearline is already calibrated to the wireless system. Now take Stew and go!"

Red whirled around to face Old Whitey. Denise and Stew jogged towards the band shell. Red strummed a chord on Pearline. "Come on, you murdering sumbitch!"

A flock of crows flying overhead cawed in support of Red's defiance.

Old Whitey smiled at Red and then looked up at the birds.

"Oh, God! No!" Red whispered.

Old Whitey returned his gaze to Red. It nodded and grinned and then blew a kiss skyward. The crows, now frozen solid, stopped in mid-flight. They hovered in the thick air for a moment and then began to rain down over Red's head. As the birds descended into Pearline's field of heat, the ice melted, leaving the dead birds heavy with moisture.

Red was caught in a rainstorm of crows. The birds battered his skull, shoulders and arms. Pearline was knocked from his hands. The guitar slid across the pavement and landed in a patch of dirt. Red stumbled and fell. "Denise! Stew," Red cried. "Pearline! Grab Pearline!"

Denise turned around and darted towards Pearline, but a piercing scream stopped her in her tracks.

"Mama!"

Denise turned in the direction of her son's cry. Old Whitey had it's cold, willowy fingers curled around Stew's neck. Stew shook violently. His skin was a pale blue.

"Stewart!" Denise rushed towards Old Whitey.

The creature held Stew off the ground with one hand. With the other hand, it slowly unzipped its fly. Old Whitey licked its snowy tongue across its lips as it leered at Denise.

A column of thick ice, in the shape of an erect penis sprung from Old Whitey's fly. The cold-beast torqued its hips powerfully. The ice-penis struck Denise in the face. Denise tumbled across the sidewalk. Her momentum came to an abrupt halt as she careened into a light pole. Denise lay still. Blood streamed from her nose and mouth.

Red struggled to his feet and then stumbled towards Pearline.

Old Whitey hurled Stew in Red's direction. The boy collided with Red's back. Red and Stew collapsed onto the pavement.

Stew raised his head slightly. "Red," He groaned. "You okay? M-mom? Where's mom?"

Red was silent. Stew looked around to check on him and found Red standing – statue still – behind him.

"Stew," Red called softly. "Run, son."

Red's eyes were as big as silver dollars. Stew looked up to see what had Red so spooked. What he saw nearly drove him to madness.

Old Whitey had transmuted itself into a massive, gaping maw several stories high. Its teeth were icy stalactites and stalagmites. Its tongue, a vortex of snow.

"Run!" Red screamed.

Stew dashed towards the band shell. Red turned and leaped towards Pearline, which was now nearly covered in snow.

The gaping maw roared and rushed forward, swallowing Red's legs in mid-leap as he bounded towards Pearline. Red stretched his arms as far as he could. He wrapped his fingers around Pearline and held her tightly as Old Whitey completely consumed him.

Stew ran into the band shell and closed the door behind him. His heart beat a drum-song in his chest. He wanted to hide somewhere and cry, but his mother needed him. Red needed him. Hell, the whole city of Chicago needed him as far as he could tell.

Stew cracked open the door and peeked out.

Old Whitey had taken the form of a naked woman, whose belly is full with child. The creature pinched its turgid ice-nipples and squeezed its snow-mound breasts. Ribbons of cold mist streamed from its tits. Old Whitey pirouetted gleefully and rubbed its rotund belly.

Stew fought the urge to vomit. "Oh, no! Red!"

Stew frantically searched the band shell until he found the mixing board, which was similar to the one at Streetwise Café, only bigger. The boy quickly examined the board.

"Here it is!"

Stew pressed a small, black button. "Come on, Red, please!"

Stew peeked outside. Old Whitey continued to prance around. To Stew, the creature looked like an expecting mom from some cold Hell.

"Red, if you're alive, please *do* something!"

Silence.

Old Whitey danced.

Tears streamed down Stew's cheeks. "Please."

A familiar tune – low and distant – tickled Stew's ear. "Is that...'Summer Breeze'? Red?"

Old Whitey stopped dancing and grimaced.

The speakers on the stage hummed. Sound exploded from them. "Yep, Summer Breeze!" Stew shouted!

Old Whitey clutched its belly and screamed in pain.

Denise, stirred by the music, rose to her knees. The music grew louder.

Old Whitey's belly split open. Red fell to the ground and continued to play furiously as the cold-creature screamed and convulsed.

Old Whitey melted away, as did snow and ice within a mile radius. The air grew balmy.

Denise threw her blood-stained coat to the ground.

Stew darted out of the band shell. By the time he reached his mother, he was sweating. "Feels like summertime!" Stew said as he held Denise tightly.

Red stood up and limped over to Stew and Denise. "It's over," he said, as he embraced them both. Old Whitey's gone!"

Denise nodded her head towards a small mound of snow behind Stew. "*Almost* gone."

Red limped over to the snow-mound. "Turn your heads."

Denise and Stew complied.

Police sirens wailed in the distance.

Red unzipped his fly and moved his hips in circles as he urinated on the mound. The snow hissed as steam rose from it.

Red paused to inspect his handiwork before limping back to Denise and Stew. "We'd better get out of here before Johnny-Law arrives."

Denise nodded. "Yeah, I wouldn't want to try to explain *this*."

"Everybody okay?" Stew asked.

The sirens grew louder.

"We'll live." Denise replied.

Stew patted Red on the arm. "So, Red, what are you doing tonight?"

Red smiled at Denise. "Checking out the Denzel version of Manchurian Candidate if the offer still stands."

"Denise grabbed the lapel of Red's safari vest, pulled him to her and pressed her soft lips to his. Denise winced as pain radiated from her lip to her left eye. "Ouch!" Denise shook her head. "That didn't go as well as I planned it, but you get the point."

Red blushed. "Yeah."

Denise and Red embraced as they laughed.

Stew clapped his hands. "Yay-uh! Don't sleep on the matchmaking skills, bay-bee!"

***

"Must have been some kids playin' around in here." A burly, ruddy-toned man shouted as he searched the band shell.

A slimmer man, but just as ruddy-skinned, peeked his head into the band shell. "Hey, Karczewski, check this out."

Officer Karczewski shuffled out of the band shell. "What ya' got, Valentine?"

Officer Valentine pointed down at the steaming mound of snow. "Looks like they just left. Whaddya think it means?"

Officer Karczewski stared down at the numbers and letters scrawled in the snow with urine. "Number four...Y...E...M...I...'Four Yemi'? Hell if *I* know. Probably some hippity-hop homeboy slang."

Officer Valentine pulverized the mound of snow with his tactical boots. "Yeah," he said with a nod. "Probably."

***

"Bruh," Z said, smiling. "Your storytellin' skills are on *fleek*!"

"On what?" Ezekiel inquired, snickering as he slid into the driver's seat of his car.

"On fleek," Z replied, hopping into the front passenger seat. "On point. How in the hell is a dude from the future *behind* the times?"

"Excuse me," Ezekiel said. "My knowledge of obscure slang ain't...on fleek."

Z's laughter was drowned out by the screech of the wheels of Ezekiel's car.

CHAPTER FIVE

"So, what's the plan?" Z asked, enjoying the feel of the wind on his face as they raced up the I-20 West highway. "How do we kill Paradox?"

"We're going to Sweet's office," Ezekiel replied. "Paradox will come after us there. Sweet has enough firepower to take Paradox out."

"Yeah...*and* a small third world country," Z said. "But ain't no way in hell you're gonna endanger my family like that!"

"They are *not* your family, Z," Ezekiel said. "And yes, I am. It's the only way you'll survive the day."

Z's fingers crept toward his pistol. "Better come up with another plan, bruh!"

Ezekiel tapped three points just beneath Z's neck with the tips of his index and middle fingers.

An intense pain shot through both of Z's hands. The teenager screamed in agony. His hand fell away from his pistol and landed in his lap, trembling uncontrollably.

"What...what did you do to me?"

"It's what I *undid* to you, actually," Ezekiel replied. "I used acupressure to numb the pain in those broken hands of yours. But the Lord giveth and the Lord taketh away."

"Well, giveth it back, Milord," Z croaked. "I promise I won't go for my weapon again."

"Right," Ezekiel said with a smirk. "I know you, son; I *am* you. The moment I fix you up, you'll go for that gun. I'd take it from you and smack you around for trying it, but I don't feel like doing all that right now, so man up and deal with that pain until we get to Sweet's."

"Bastard!" Z spat.

"Yep," Ezekiel said, smiling.

*****

The pain in Z's hands grew unbearable. His vision blurred and an ocean of sickness ebbed and flowed in his gut.

Through the dense fog of anguish he saw the sign on the glass double doors – *Sweet South Records*.

"Please, mister...don't do this," Z said, a line of spittle running from the corner of his mouth to his chin. "Sweet is like a father to me."

"That daddy of yours is the reason I'm here," Ezekiel said. "He's the reason why Grandfather Paradox is here. He sent me back in time in an experiment in time travel. Made me a guinea pig because I committed the sin of wanting to go straight; to raise a family. Sweet wants to know how time really works...well, I'm about to show him."

"No!" Z spat. I'm gonna..."

The ocean of sickness churned. A tidal wave crashed in Z's gut and spewed out of his mouth. The car seemed to whirl hither and thither. Z closed his eyes and submitted to the darkness that blanketed him.

CHAPTER SIX

A scream, more pained than one issued in the throes of childbirth, jolted Z out of his oblivion. He inhaled, bracing himself for the pain that would surely follow his next move. He slipped the twisted fingers of his right hand behind the door handle and then pressed his left forearm against the back of his right hand. He pushed. White-hot pain shot through his fingers. He grunted, fighting the urge to cry out.

The door opened a crack.

Z leaned away from the door, raised his foot and kicked it open wide. He climbed out of the car and trotted up to the doors of Sweet's office building, thanking the heavens that they were automatic as they slid open.

He sprinted inside, ran past the elevator – not wanting to waste time awaiting it – and then bounded up the stairs.

When he reached the third floor – the floor upon which Sweet's and Norm's offices were located – a powerful stench of salt, metal and meat assaulted him. He gingerly pulled the door open and then peeked into the hallway. The walls were painted with blood and flesh – a mural of red, pink and brown.

A tableau of suited bodies lay twisted and torn along the length of the hall.

Z stumbled past the bodies until he reached Sweet's office. A headless body in a white suit lay slumped across Sweet's desk. Nigerian Norm lay dead at the front of the desk. His massive muscles seemed somehow loose on his broken frame.

Z heard rapid breathing to his left. He whirled toward the noise.

In the corner of the office, sitting on his haunches, was Ezekiel. Blood poured from the side of his head and only a jagged hole remained where his right eye once was.

Z leapt toward him and launched a hard front kick into the man's face.

"Didn't feel a thing, kiddo," Ezekiel said. "My back's broken, I think."

"Why?" Z cried. "Why did you do this?"

"So we get a second chance, son," Ezekiel replied. "Through you. Me dying sets time back right. Sweet dying sets *you* right. You don't have to worry about Paradox – or Sweet's paradoxical ass anymore."

"But he was family."

"Go home, kid," Ezekiel said. "Your mother needs you. You need her. Go home!"

"I guess I got no choice," Z whispered.

"Nope," Ezekiel replied. "Oh, and here!"

Ezekiel flicked his wrist weakly. A shiny object flew out of his hands.

Z reached out both palms and let the object fall into them. It was an expensive-looking watch.

"Take that and hide it," Ezekiel said. "One day, you'll be able to sell the technology inside it for a mint."

"A watch?" Z said, shaking his head. "Watches have been around since forever."

"Not *that* kind of watch," Ezekiel replied.

"Well, it *is* kinda cool the way it's glowing," Z said.

"Glowing? No!" Ezekiel gasped.

"Yeah," Z said outstretching his palms toward Ezekiel's face. The face of the watch glowed neon blue. "See?"

"No!" Ezekiel shouted. "Toss it! Toss it, now!"

"Why?" Z asked. "It's just..."

The room went white.

Ezekiel slumped over onto his side. Through his one good eye he saw Z vanish.

"Welcome to my world, kid," he coughed. "Welcome to my world."

ABOUT THE AUTHOR

Balogun is the author of the bestselling *Afrikan Martial Arts: Discovering the Warrior Within* and *The Afrikan Warriors' Bible* and screenwriter / producer / director of the films, *A Single Link, Rite of Passage: Initiation* and *Rite of Passage: The Dentist of Westminster*.

He is one of the leading authorities on Steamfunk – a philosophy or style of writing that combines the African and / or African American culture and approach to life with that of the steampunk philosophy and / or steampunk fiction – and writes about it, the craft of writing, Sword & Soul and Steampunk in general, at http://chroniclesofharriet.com/.

He is author of eight novels – the Steamfunk bestseller, *MOSES: The Chronicles of Harriet Tubman (Books 1 & 2)*; the Urban Science Fiction saga, *Redeemer*; the Sword & Soul epic, *Once Upon A Time In Afrika*; a Fight Fiction, New Pulp novella, *Fist of Afrika*; the gritty, Urban Superhero series, *A Single Link* and *Wrath of the Siafu*; the two-fisted Dieselfunk tale, *The Scythe* and the

"Choose-Your-Own-Destiny"-style Young Adult novel, *The Keys*. Balogun is also contributing co-editor of two anthologies: *Ki: Khanga: The Anthology* and *Steamfunk*.

Finally, Balogun is the Director and Fight Choreographer of the Steamfunk feature film, *Rite of Passage*, which he wrote based on the short story, *Rite of Passage*, by author Milton Davis and co-author of the award winning screenplay, *Ngolo*.

You can reach him on Facebook at facebook.com/Afrikan.Martial.Arts; on Twitter at twitter.com/Baba_Balogun and on Tumblr at tumblr.com/blog/blackspeculativefiction.

www.ingramcontent.com/pod-product-compliance
Lightning Source LLC
Chambersburg PA
CBHW050904250626

47155CB00001B/97